Plastic
Angel

Nerissa Nields

SCHOLASTIC INC.
New York Toronto London Auckland Sydney
Mexico City New Delhi Hong Kong Buenos Aires

ACKNOWLEDGMENTS

Thanks to my writing and guitar students who constantly inspire me with their creativity and their curiosity. Thanks to my audience: You have faith to move mountains. Thanks to all those who read various drafts of this ever-changing work: Katryna Nields, Sheila Turner, Abigail Nields, my parents, Gail and John Nields, Tom Duffy, Dave Chalfant, Patty Romanoff, and Nalini Jones. Thanks to Anna Kirwan and the Tuesday night group, and then thanks again to Anna Kirwan. Thanks to Randi Reisfeld, my inspired editor, and to Joy Peskin and Rachel Klein Lisberg. Thanks to my agent, Ginger Knowlton, and to her assistant Kelly Going. Thanks to John Virant. Thanks to Kristen Walton for the authentic Britishisms. Thanks to Billy Blake for the plastic angel. Thanks to Dar Williams for telling me there would be no better use of my time than to write a novel. Thanks to all those angels who sustain me by tiny threads, which they may not even be aware of holding.

And thanks most of all to you for reading this.

And one more thanks to Katryna and Patty.

The complete soundtrack for this book is a CD called *This Town Is Wrong* by Nerissa & Katryna Nields. It is available on Rounder / Zoë Records and at www.nields.com.

This book was originally published in hardcover by Orchard Books in 2005.

ISBN 0-439-51996-9

Text copyright © 2005 by Nerissa Nields.
All rights reserved. Published by Scholastic Inc.
SCHOLASTIC and associated logos are trademarks
and/or registered trademarks of Scholastic Inc.

12 11 10 9 8 7 6 5 4 3 2 1   5 6 7 8 9 10/0

Printed in the U.S.A.   40

First Scholastic paperback printing, October 2005

The text type was set in 12-point CG Collage.

Book design by Kristina Albertson

For Amelia and Reese
and their mothers,
Katryna and Abigail

CHAPTER ONE

is She a Goddess or What?

I can see them now. Two of my friends from school are hunched over a computer, compiling a list. Not just *a* list, mind you. *The* List. The List that everyone at Clairman Country Day School lives and dies by.

Shawna Gilbert and Essie Reynolds are poised right about now above my name.

"Randi Rankin?" Shawna yawns, one well-manicured finger suspended above the keyboard.

"Randi? Randi's one of us," Essie says, looking over Shawna's shoulder.

Shawna rolls her eyes. "*Was*. We've got to reassess now that it's summer vacation. It's a whole new season, Essie.

Out with the old, in with the new. And everyone knows the summer between eighth and ninth grades is the time when people go from geek to chic. Or the other way around. And, if you ask me, Randi's right on the edge."

"What edge?" says Essie, concerned.

"Have you noticed how much time Randi spends with that weirdo Gellie Riddle? In fact, do you know where Randi is right this second? She's at the Are You a Goddess competition at the mall. Watching Gellie make a total fool of herself. I told Randi, too. I said, 'We like you, but some people think you're kind of boring.' I offered to help her. You know, like, as her handler. And my first tip? Lose Gellie."

"But Randi's nice," says Essie, the nicer of the two. She's trying to make it sound as though "nice" trumps "bad taste in friends."

They're both right. I am nice. And everyone knows "nice" means "boring." It's not just how other people see me. It's how I see me. And I don't want to go through one more year being boring. I don't want to go through one more year being the nice kid who never quite makes The List.

I do spend a lot of time with Gellie, whose real name is Angela. Her family calls her Gellie, and once the boys in school got wind of that, it was "Peanut Butter And" twenty-four-seven.

In school she is an outcast. But she's my friend. My best friend, maybe.

And here in JCPenney at the Clairman Mall, she's a star.

Gellie is beautiful. Professionally beautiful, that is. The only reason I'm here is because of Gellie. I cannot begin to tell you how much teen-modeling contests are not my thing. They are my anti-thing. But she made me promise to go with her.

☆ ☆ ☆

"And now. Imagine how good you'll feel cuddled up with your cutie in front of a raging fire out on the slopes next winter! In a chartreuse ski parka with flame-thrower zipper, here's Emily Higgins. Is she a goddess or WHAT?"

The emcee for this event, a pert woman with a blond ponytail and high-heeled sneakers, says, "Is she a goddess or what?" to introduce each of the twelve girls as they parade down the runway. She has one of those high nasal voices to go with her high-heeled sneakers and hair-sprayed high ponytail. A scared-looking red-haired girl comes forward, modeling winter clothes even though it's early June.

Gellie's mom, Mrs. Riddle, has come from behind the rows of clothes where she was getting Gellie ready and sits down next to me, barely looking my way. Half the time, she seems to like me well enough, but every now and then, she looks at me as if she doesn't quite know how I got into her life. I think it's because of my parents. They're kind of oddballs in Clairman. My mom is just starting up her business as an acupuncturist. She's set up an office in our house. My dad, Guy Rankin, is a professional singer–songwriter who's been almost famous ever since

I was a baby. He's out touring a lot and so far has had only one big hit. It's because of him that I love music. In Clairman, if you're an almost-famous singer-songwriter, you're definitely an oddball.

Mrs. Riddle is another kind of oddball. She and Gellie have always been joined at the hip, running all over town wherever there's a chance for a spotlight to shine on Gellie.

Gellie lives across the street from me. Shawna and Essie don't know that she's my best friend for a fact. But they know enough. They know that hanging out with Gellie lowers my cool-in-school status. Being popular is what it's all about for Shawna and Essie. If Shawna and Essie got to know her, they might even like her eventually. But not now. Now they're totally fixated on The List.

The prettiest girl is never the most popular. In fact, being anything "the most" is always bad. You can't be too tall, too short, too fat, too thin, too smart, too dumb. And Gellie is too everything. She's the shortest, the thinnest, the smartest, plus there's that whole modeling thing. And she doesn't do herself any favors. She can come off as acting sort of above it all.

"The Wild West is alive and well today, thanks in part to fabulous footwear that never goes out of fashion! Wearing camel sand boots and ready to ride, here's ANGELA RIDDLE. Is she a goddess or what?"

Gellie comes forward like a pro, swinging her hips and smiling a little half smile. She's a completely different person on the runway from who she is anywhere else. At school, she's a folded piece of paper, rail thin, two-dimensional. At home, she's the baby of the family, doted on by her mother, picked on by her older sisters, Margie and Barbara. But this Gellie, the girl I see onstage at JCPenney, is powerful. There's something about her that makes it impossible not to look at her, and it's more than just her beauty. I look around, and I notice that everyone has stopped talking and is fixated on Gellie. She looks like a rock star.

She swishes by me and turns on a dime, perfectly balanced and full of grace. Her heart-shaped face glows underneath the layers of makeup Mrs. Riddle put on her. Her long hair, which she usually wears pulled into a simple ponytail, fans out like there's an air machine blowing it back. She's wearing a suede miniskirt with her camel sand boots, and she looks about ten years older than she is. Anything but two-dimensional.

From the day we moved to Clairman when I was nine years old, I've dreamed of getting back to Jintucket, Massachusetts, the town where I was born. I think Clairman is responsible for the boring-ization of me, Randi Rankin.

Mom made us leave Jintucket when she found her dream house in Clairman, the one she'd been waiting for her whole life. But how can her dream house be located in the world's most boring town? In Clairman, all the houses are white with green shutters. It's a town ordinance or something.

Dad feels the same way about Clairman that I do. If the motto in Jintucket is Be Who You Are, the motto in Clairman should be Be Who We Tell You to Be. My dad was born in Jintucket. My mom comes from Ohio. In addition to the whole "dream house" argument, Mom was concerned about the unstructured school I went to in Jintucket. She was worried I'd never get into college, never learn the basics. So she took all the money she and Dad had and put me in this private school, Clairman Country Day. And we moved into her dream house on Raglan Road in Clairman, across the road from Gellie Riddle and her family.

Our house is right up against the road; it's a white clap-board farmhouse with — big surprise — green shutters. It's a small but very cozy version of every other house in town. The Riddles' house is a huge version of the standard Clairman house. It's like a giant at the end of a long driveway.

Mom loves everything about our house except the road. It's what takes Dad away from us. She always seems to forget that it's also what brings him home again.

☆ ☆ ☆

"That little one is a cutie," I hear the women in front of me say. "The one with the cowboy boots? She's going places, I tell you."

"Oh, yeah, isn't she the Face of Clairman girl?" says the other woman.

It's true. Gellie is The Face of Clairman. When you drive into town, there's a gigantic billboard saying WELCOME TO CLAIRMAN with Gellie's face smiling down on you.

Gellie's been a model for all sorts of products her whole life. Adults come up to her in the supermarket, holding jars of peanut butter and pointing to the smiling six-year-old on the front. They say, "Your little face is still on the label of this! Oh, it brings me right back, to see you still so young! And you look just the same!"

I'm sure this makes the Peanut Butter And joke even more painful.

She's almost famous the way I'm almost popular. You'd think being almost famous would *make* her popular. Somehow it doesn't, no more than being almost popular would make me famous.

After the last girl models a light-green sweater vest with a sky-blue wool hat, I watch the emcee speak with the judges. She comes to the front of the runway and announces that Gellie is Clairman's new Goddess. All the girls hug each other, like they do at beauty pageants. Gellie's mom leaps to her feet and screams, "Brava, *brava*!"

And then Mrs. Riddle turns to me and exclaims, "Do you know what this means? This means we might have a shot at getting a real agent! And if we get a real agent, Gellie is going to get a huge boost for her career. I predict this win will be the turning point. Gellie is going to have a very busy summer!"

And she hurries over to Gellie, a glowing star for the moment, completely in her element. I have to admit, Gellie's got something pretty amazing here, even if I happen to think it's totally goofy and bound to keep her from having a social life. I sort of get why she keeps modeling. It must be fun to have everyone fawn all over you.

☆ ☆ ☆

On the back of the paper program for the Are You a Goddess contest, I make my own list. About what would be fun for me.

IT WOULD BE FUN TO BE ON THE LIST.

I want to stay friends with Shawna and Essie and their crowd and to have them see me as one of them. But they think I'm boring.

IT WOULD BE FUN NOT TO BE BORING.

I chew on my pencil. Something my dad always says comes back to me. "Do what you love most and you'll never be bored."

Maybe if I'm not bored, I won't be boring.

IT WOULD BE FUN TO MAKE MUSIC.

I'm a good singer. I'm learning to play the guitar. Dad gave me an acoustic for Christmas, along with a note that said GOOD FOR FIVE GUITAR LESSONS. He's out touring all the time, so we've only had four lessons in six months. He taught me the basic chords and I learned them right away. I even wrote a song. Well, the beginning of a song.

It's really terrible, and it came out all shapeless, like a dress with no waist, with tons of verses and no chorus.

IT WOULD BE FUN TO MAKE MUSIC WITH GELLIE.

I WANT TO START A ROCK BAND. WITH GELLIE.

Gellie's a good writer. She gets As in Creative Writing. She's also really beautiful. I'm just kind of normal looking. With Gellie in my band, we'll be huge. You have to have at least one beautiful person in a band to make it. That's what Dad says.

And suddenly, the answer I didn't even know I was looking for comes to me. It'll solve everything. If we're in a band together, everyone will respect Gellie and me. We'll get invited to all the parties, and cute guys will ask us out. No one will call her Peanut Butter And. And no one will think I'm boring.

I look at my list and then at Gellie's glowing Goddess face. All I have to do is find a way to convince her.

CHAPTER TWO

Lessons

"OK, my little Glory, listen closely," says Dad. We are sitting on the back porch. The June sun is still high in the sky, but it's not quite as hot as it's been all day long. Dad's got his old Martin guitar on his lap, and I have my brand-new Takamine. He's going to teach me my first barre chord: F-sharp minor. I'm learning one thing quickly: Barre chords involve a lot of pain.

"Press down as hard as you can," he says, holding his left hand over mine. I'm struggling to cover all six strings with my left index finger while at the same time using my third, fourth, and fifth fingers to make the shape for the chord. When I strum the strings with my right hand, it sounds dead and muffled. Gagged. I try again and it's even worse.

"I hate this!"

"Just keep at it," says Dad. "The thing about barre chords is, they sound terrible for weeks and months, until one day when — out of the blue — you sit down with your guitar and suddenly you can play a barre chord. It'll be as though you were born playing them. But you have to keep practicing."

He lets go of my left hand, and he strums his own guitar, playing my enemy, F-sharp minor, and making it reverberate through the neighborhood. Then he raises his eyebrows and gestures with his hands toward me and my guitar as if to say, "Go ahead, *you* try it." I immediately start strumming as fast as I can. Since our last lesson, I figured out a whole ton of songs that use just three chords. Now I can play "All Day and All of the Night" by The Kinks.

Dad looks concerned.

"Be careful or someone's going to think you're playing 'Hello I Love You' by The Doors. In this house, The Doors are not welcome." Then he gets that look on his face that means he's about to tell a terrible joke. "Our doors are closed to The Doors!"

I roll my eyes.

"Come on," says Dad, nudging me. "That was partly funny! At least sixty percent! Give me at least a chuckle!"

You actually might have heard of my dad. Guy Rankin. He wrote that song "Kiss Me on the Moon." Jenne

Teasbury sang it. It was a pretty big hit about eleven years ago when I was two. Mom says we're still living off those royalties. Mostly, Dad writes songs for women singers, since "Kiss Me on the Moon" was a hit for a woman. So it's sort of weird when he sings them. I wish he'd write from his own point of view.

I'm the only kid at school with a musician dad. Maybe that's why I'm almost accepted by the popular kids.

On the other hand, people think my acupuncturist mom and musician dad are weird. Everyone else has parents who are bankers or lawyers or doctors or have some business that doesn't involve guitars and needles. Maybe in trying to seem normal, I come across as blah. Maybe that's why Shawna said I was boring.

But back to the guitar lesson.

"The most important thing I can tell you about playing guitar is that it's all about the *feel*. It's not about getting every note right. It's not about playing perfectly in rhythm. It's about knowing when to slow down, when to speed up just a hair, when to dig in, and when to lay back. That's what sets apart the Beatles or Bob Dylan from all those yokels you've never heard of. Present company excluded," he says, clearing his throat. "Listen. I'll show you."

And he pulls a pick from his back pocket and starts to sing. Then he suddenly stops.

"Sing the rest of the song," I say.

"*You* sing it," he says. "What kind of a guitar lesson would this be if I sang every song?"

"Come on," I say. "I'll sing harmony."

"I'll tell you what," he says. "Let me show you the chords to the chorus, and then *you* can play and *I'll* sing. I already know you can harmonize. This is a *guitar* lesson. Remember?"

I'm really good at harmony. I'm only an OK singer, but ever since I was a little kid, I've had this weird gift of being able to sing a different tune along with my dad. And the tune somehow fits with the other person's tune. I didn't know there was a name for this until I heard my father say to Aunt Izzie once, "Randi can sing perfect harmonies to any song you throw at her."

I know, compared to Gellie being so smart and a Goddess and almost famous and all, it isn't much. Still, it's something.

I'm not as talented yet with the guitar.

"I can't do this!" I shout, banging a C chord on my guitar. "I give up!"

Dad bangs a G chord on his. "Yeah! Me, too! I am *so* angry that after all these years, I still can't play like Carlos Santana! It's so unfair! I never should have picked up the guitar! I quit!"

I giggle in spite of myself.

"What's so funny out here?" asks Mom, coming to the door. As soon as she opens it, our cats, Roy and Leo, shoot out into the backyard.

"Our little Glory," says Dad. "As usual, she wants to race ahead before she's learned the whole game. But," he adds, tousling my hair, "she's going to knock 'em dead once she can get her barre chords down."

"My fingers kill," I moan, holding up my left hand to show Mom the grooves on the tips. She takes my hand and kisses each finger.

"Come on in, you two," she says. "Kung pao chicken for dinner."

☆ ☆ ☆

"How was your day?" Dad asks Mom, passing me the rice. It's red. Mom's been into weird food recently. Last week we had black rice and fiddlehead ferns.

"Good," she says. "I treated a patient for anxiety. I opened up the Gate of Opportunity point on her central meridian and her chi changed and started to flow beautifully."

Dad puts a little rice on his plate and then twice as much kung pao chicken. "I'll never understand how sticking a needle into someone could actually be relaxing," he says. "I guess all that needlepoint you used to do is finally paying off." He looks up at Mom and grins. Dad's always teasing us that way, but tonight Mom doesn't smile back.

Mom's just started her business, and we recently made Dad's recording studio into Mom's acupuncture office. She even has two regular patients now. Dad's new studio is the old linen closet. You can barely even sit down in there. But Dad does, because sometimes from behind the closed door I can hear him playing his guitar. Sometimes I take a book and sit outside the door and read while I listen to him play. When Dad's home, the house is always full of music, either his own or someone else's, coming from the ratty old stereo speakers he hung on the living room wall. Dad's been on the road a lot this spring, playing backup guitar for a country singer named Gayle Al Fresca. You can't imagine how quiet the house is when he's not here.

But now the house is quiet and he *is* here. Mom and Dad are eating and not talking to each other.

"What's Shawna doing this summer?" Mom asks me finally. My mom loves Shawna. She thinks Shawna is "a solid kid and a good influence." I think she just likes the fact that Shawna's parents went to Princeton, the school Mom worships and wants me to get into.

"She's going to be babysitting for her neighbors. They have triplets."

"Good money in that, I bet," says Dad. "I'm assuming she gets three times the regular fee."

"Honey, that's something *you* could do," Mom says suddenly. She and I have been circling around the issue of What Randi Should Do This Summer for weeks. She doesn't really care about me making money. She just wants me to have some structure so she doesn't have to worry about me and instead can concentrate on her business. Meanwhile, I keep changing the subject, hoping I can make it till late August without a summer job. I can't tell you how much I don't want to work in the summertime. After all the misery of the school year, I deserve a break!

"What's Gellie up to?" says Dad. Sometimes Gellie comes over and she and Dad compare notes on being almost famous. Neither of them is the kind of famous where you're a household name. But both of them, every once in a while, have some stranger come up to them and say, "Don't I know you from somewhere?" Of course, no one shoves peanut butter jars in Dad's face. Yet.

"The usual," I say, my mouth full of rice and chicken. "She just won the Are You a Goddess competition. At the mall. It was truly horrific."

Dad nods.

"I think it's great that you're incorporating her more into your group," says Mom. "I've been worried about that child for years. She has no social life at all, outside of all those modeling competitions."

Dad adds, "And those horrible commercials the poor kid had to do. That was a disaster."

Even my parents see that Gellie's life is dominated by her mother and the stupid things she gets Gellie to do. The worst ever was this commercial for this toy company, Fiskel. They had this idea to make huge, ugly plastic jewelry for little girls. The pieces Gellie showed me, the prototypes, she called them, were hideous. One was a giant yellow flower with a little talking cat in the center of the petals. One was a pink-and-aqua-beaded necklace with sparkly fake diamonds in each bead. I think maybe more than anything, this was what completely wrecked Gellie socially.

"Wasn't there something about ordering special beads online with your friends' names or photographs on them or something?" says Dad. "Maybe I should tell my agent to get me a deal with Fiskel. Guy Rankin necklaces for Guy Rankin fans."

"It was sort of a smart idea," says Mom after a moment, ignoring Dad. "Like those add-a-bead necklaces in the 1980s."

"Huh?" I say.

"Never mind. I'm just saying, it's kind of a good idea. You have all your friends' pictures hanging around your neck. Sort of like a locket. A cross between a charm bracelet and a locket. A charm locket." She says this with her eyebrows raised and a big smile, the kind of smile moms give you when they think they've thought of a really great idea for you.

"I guess," I say.

"Those necklaces were huge, though," says Dad. "I always thought you'd throw out your back just wearing them around. Can you imagine how you'd feel if your bead was the bead that made your friend finally keel over?"

Dad and I laugh. But Mom is hot for this charm-locket idea.

"Randi, that's it! You can have your own business making charm lockets! Yours would be much better than those plastic ones."

"Mom," I say, rolling my eyes. "Do you think I'm eight

years old? You want me to spend my summer doing arts and crafts? Forget it. I'm going to start a rock band this summer. That's going to keep me busy."

Both of them put down their chopsticks and stare at me but for different reasons.

"Well, it's about time," crows Dad. "My little Glory! A chip off the old rock!"

"Hold on just a second," says Mom. "The last thing I need is to have a garage full of teenagers making a racket while I'm trying to treat a patient. I knew I should've focused on this. Guy, I've been telling you we needed to figure out Randi's summer. I told you I needed your help on this one. I have to concentrate on starting up my practice!"

My mom's the kind of person who gets mad at everyone else as soon as she feels like she's screwed something up. Tonight's no exception. She is glaring at both of us, but my dad gets the full fire of her eyes.

"Come on, Madeleine," he says, giving up on trying to balance the peanuts on his chopsticks and instead using his fingers. "She wants to make music. I think it's great."

"You *would* think it's great," she fumes. "You get to brag to all your musician pals that you have a daughter who's following in your footsteps. Meanwhile, I get to drive her to rehearsals and gigs and . . ."

"Oh, relax. She's not going to have gigs for years," says Dad.

"Well," says Mom sputtering, clearly feeling ganged up on.

"Mom!" I shout. "You won't have to drive me anywhere. The only other person I want in my band is Gellie. We can rehearse at her house."

I get up from the table and stick my plate in the sink. There's too much tension between Mom and Dad, and I know if I stick around it'll just get worse, since it's obviously about me. It's sometimes better if they just go ahead and have a fight, just like it's sometimes better when you have the flu to go ahead and throw up. But that doesn't mean I need to be here for it.

"Wait a second, Glory," says Dad. "I have an idea. Madeleine, you might like this, too. What if I can get Randi a job at Real Tunes working for my friend John. He can use her help in the stockroom or helping customers or even just putting price stickers on CDs."

Ka-ching! John is Mr. Supreme Hottie, if you ask me.

Mom goes to the sink and starts doing the dishes, and I know that means she likes the plan but isn't ready to stop being mad at both of us. I go over to her and put my head on her shoulder and my arms around her waist. This is what smart daughters do.

"Please, Mom," I whisper. "I promise I'll be the quietest rock and roller ever. And I'll ride my bike to Real Tunes."

And I feel her giggle. She turns around and hugs me without getting her wet hands on me. She has a special talent for that.

"Well, OK. It sounds like a good plan, actually."

"You're the coolest mom ever," I say, running up the stairs to e-mail Gellie.

"Don't stay up too late," calls Mom.

"Yeah," says Dad. "And don't forget to practice those barre chords."

I lean over the banister and hold up my left index finger, wiggling it weakly.

"No problem," I say. "If the feeling ever returns to this part of my body."

I don't have my own computer. Dad lets me use his for schoolwork, but it makes him nervous when I go online. He's paranoid that if I do, all his recordings will be destroyed. Once or twice when I've been online, his computer has crashed, but he never loses anything. He always thinks he will, though. Parents can sort of lose it when it comes to computers. They get all frantic. "Wait, wait! Did you save that?" they're always saying, looking over my shoulder when I'm trying to help them out. Anyway, the point is, when I want to e-mail Gellie, I have to sneak. When Dad's home, it's harder to do this, and sometimes I go for days without getting to check my e-mail. It's really annoying. I've explained to my parents over and over that having your own computer is more important than having a coat or books, but they just roll their eyes at me.

"Just because you go to school with a bunch of rich kids doesn't mean you have to have every ridiculous bourgeois luxury they have," says Dad. "Writing with good old pen and paper builds character!"

But when I open my e-mail, there's one from Gellie.

> Dear Randi,
> I want to celebrate my big victory in Jintucket tomorrow. Will you come with me? I'll buy you a froyo at Yogi Dave's with the $$$ I won for being a Goddess. Pleaseoplease?
> Your rich friend,
> Gellie

But before I can reply, I hear Dad shouting, "Are you on the computer?" so I retreat to The Sanctuary, aka my room.

I have a lava lamp with a red-velvet-framed photo of Mom. My white wooden bureau is covered with photos, letters, notes, stickers, and pictures from magazines. Also a bunch of quotations I like:

> *It is a curious thought, but it is only when you see people looking ridiculous that you realize just how much you love them.* — AGATHA CHRISTIE
> *Keep away from people who try to belittle your ambitions. Small people always do that, but the really great make you feel that you, too, can become great.* — MARK TWAIN
> *When did dress up turn to fashion?* — DAR WILLIAMS

A postcard of Emily Dickinson, my favorite poet, is on the wall. I stuck a Post-it next to it, with one of her couplets:

Hope is the thing with feathers
That perches in the soul,
And sings the tune without the words
And never stops at all.

I hung a string of lights with silver sparkly stars above my window. Stars are my thing. I've had glow-in-the-dark stars on my ceiling ever since I was born. Dad put new ones in this room when we moved here. This is probably the one groovy place in the entire town of Clairman. I should charge admission.

Roy is curled up next to me on the bed. I pick up my guitar off the carpet. I want to play "Kiss Me on the Moon," but I can only play part of it.

Still, I get up and strap my guitar over my shoulder with the sun-and-moon-and-stars guitar strap Aunt Izzie gave me. I sing the parts I learned today in front of my full-length mirror. With a guitar in front of me, I look about ten years older. I go to bed and dream about working at Real Tunes with John. Except in my dream, John looks and sounds exactly like Carlos Santana.

CHAPTER THREE

Place-Saver Boyfriends

Jintucket is just seven miles from Clairman, but it's the longest seven miles I know.

Bright colors are everywhere across the bridge in Jintucket. Even if a person is wearing all black, his hair at least will be pink or green. Even the dogs in Jintucket are more interesting. Jintucket is famous for Mutts on Purpose, a puppy farm where they breed all sorts of crazy mixes: dachshunds crossed with Akitas, border collies crossed with pugs, and my favorite, poodles crossed with wolfhounds. In Clairman, there are two acceptable dog breeds: golden retrievers and Labrador retrievers. In Clairman, everyone's dressed like they just stepped out of a J. Crew catalog. There must be some city ordinance stating that teenage girls need to be tall, thin, and blonde. I'm in violation of that ordinance. So's Gellie, come to think of it, though I bet that never occurred to Mrs. Riddle.

Gellie and I park our bikes on the bike rack in front of Yogi Dave's Frozen Yogurt Shop. We each get frozen yogurt — white chocolate for her, blueberry for me — and eat as we walk down the street. There's not a cloud in the sky, and the leaves are fresh and green on the trees. Everyone's out on the street, dressed in colorful, outrageous clothes. It's like a carnival. People are pushing strollers or walking their funny mutts on homemade leashes. *Sgt. Pepper's Lonely Hearts Club Band* is playing from the speakers Yogi Dave just hung in the trees in front of the storefront, announcing the beginning of summer. I nod at a couple walking by. I remember them vaguely from growing up here; I think they went to the meditation hall Mom and Dad used to go to. They smile and wave hello. "Say hi to Guy and Madeleine for us, will you?" they holler as they cross the street. I can't wait till I get to live here again. Everything about this town is right. Everything about Clairman is wrong.

"Let's go by Real Tunes," I say. "I think I'm going to try to get a summer job there."

"A summer job?" says Gellie, joking. "What's that? I'll never have a summer job. All I ever do is model clothes."

"That pays a lot more than working in a music store," I point out.

"Yeah, but between auditioning for the modeling jobs and getting them, I never even have time to breathe," says Gellie. "Sometimes I just want to do something normal like babysit or work in a store. Speaking of which, we need to go to Hillary's Hipper. Don't tell my mom, but I want to get that yellow T-shirt with the monkey face on it. She said it made me look slutty. But I thought it was cool."

"It *was* cool," I say. For a model, Gellie has terrible clothes. Her nice things are stiff and uncomfortable and even if she did want to wear them, her mother would never let her, unless it was to a job. So instead, she wears hand-me-downs from her sisters — Margie's baggy clothes or Barbara's preppy tailored things. We walk past Atticus Books and Bibi's Boutique and look in the window of Real Tunes. John is behind the counter, as usual. He's tall and skinny and has red hair and a beard and the gentlest brown eyes you've ever seen. He's from London. He plays guitar and keeps his finger on the pulse of the local music scene. He always shows me the rare imports and tells me which new CDs to get.

John has been getting over a broken heart. His girl-friend, Kate, didn't ever make it over from England, though when he first moved here, it seemed like she would any day. "In about a month," he'd say whenever I asked. But she always had some delay. One day, I came into the store to buy Gillian Welch's new record, and he was sitting on his stool behind the counter, sadder than anyone I've ever seen. He was playing Bob Dylan's *Blood on the Tracks*. To be more accurate, he had the song "You're a Big Girl Now" on perpetual repeat. But today he is playing house music from the early 1990s, which means he's probably in a good mood.

"When's your dad coming home?" he asks, moving a stack of CDs over to the bins and filing them alphabetically. John's a fan. He always makes sure Dad's bin is full.

"He got back last week, actually," I say.

"Who was he out with again?"

"Gayle Al Fresca," I tell him, rolling my eyes. Gayle is really young and beautiful, and her record company, Juno, is pumping all sorts of money and promotion into her latest CD, *Fresh from the Farm*. Personally, I can't stand her, and I hate the way Dad is always talking about trying to get her to cover his songs. It's demeaning. But Mom says it pays the bills.

"Oh, yeah, her," says John. "Her record company just sent me loads of posters to put up. *She's* a looker."

I ignore that. "This is my friend Gellie," I say.

He sticks out his hand, very mock-formal. "Pleased to make your acquaintance, Miss Jellybean. Any friend of the distinguished Miss Rankin is a friend of mine."

And he rests his hand on my shoulder. His touch makes my knees go weak. I know that sounds totally cliché and out of some romance novel or something, but it's true.

"See you later," I mumble and drag Gellie out of the store. The sun hurts my eyes after the dark of the record store.

"You didn't talk about working for him," notes Gellie.

"Oh, yeah," I say. "Well, my dad says he'll call him." I am out of breath, even though we haven't even walked five paces.

"What's wrong with you?"

"I don't know." Then I sigh. "I think he's so amazing, I can hardly stand to be in the same room with him."

Gellie frowns. "He's too old for you."

"So? I can still dream, can't I?"

Gellie looks at me sideways and opens her mouth and then closes it again as though she's decided it's better not to say anything. But I keep pushing it.

"At least I fantasize about guys rather than completely ignore them, like you do!"

"I do not ignore them!"

"You do so! What about you and Duge? He is madly in love with you."

Terry Duganton is otherwise known as Duge, which rhymes with "huge." He's the smallest kid in the school. He has hair that sticks straight up because of all his cowlicks. "Fourteen," he told me. "I counted them once."

Duge thinks he's the students' ambassador to the faculty at Clairman Country Day. To call him a teacher's pet would be an understatement. Everybody loves him or, at least, treats him with fear and respect. He somehow finds out every secret anyone has, including all of the teachers'. He knows things about me before I do. He's also really smart. He's an international spy waiting to happen.

"I don't have time for *Duge*," Gellie says curtly, her eyes on her feet, moving faster toward Hillary's Hipper. "And maybe I don't have time for boys right this second. I have too much to do. I can barely see *you* this summer. My mom's got me entered in a competition or signed up for an audition every week, sometimes twice a week."

I guess now is not the time to bring up my idea of starting a rock band.

We go into Hillary's Hipper, a fun, cheap clothing store. There are red carpets on the walls instead of the floors and tapestries hanging from the ceiling, along with Japanese lanterns. Gellie pulls out a pair of red-striped pants from the rack and holds them up to her chest.

"What do you think about these?"

Before I can answer, someone else does for me.

"Yeah, those would look great on you."

I turn and see Shawna Gilbert and Essie Reynolds.

Shawna is talking. "Essie, those are the exact pants you wore in fourth grade, remember?"

"Shut *up*," says Essie, laughing and giving Shawna a little shove. "I don't *think* so!"

Gellie puts the pants back on the rack.

"*Kidding*," says Shawna. "How are you guys? I was just thinking about you."

She says this more to me. I'm kind of shocked to see them here. I can't imagine either of them wearing Hillary's clothes. They're more the Abercrombie types.

"Good," I say, trying to act like nothing vicious just happened. "What are you guys doing here?"

"Getting something to wear to my retro party," says Essie. "This Saturday. You should come, Randi." As she says this, she kind of tilts her shoulder toward me and away from Gellie. Essie is short, though not as short as Gellie, with corn-silk blond hair that never gets frizzy in humidity the way mine does. She has a ski-jump nose. She almost never gets zits, and she wears clothes no more than two months old. Her father is president of the I-Tech Corporation and drives a Jaguar. Her mother designs place mats. Essie's name is really Sarah Catherine, but her parents called her S.C. Our fifth-grade teacher thought it was "Essie," which Essie liked better than S.C., so now that's how we all spell it. It looks really pretty when you write it out in cursive.

As for Shawna, she's practically got an entire cult built around her at Clairman Country Day. She's got dark glossy hair and the longest legs I've ever seen. When I first moved to Clairman, she took me under her wing. We used to act out the entire story of *The Little Mermaid*. Only she knew the Disney version and I knew the Hans Christian Andersen version, so we'd always fight over whether the little mermaid lived or died at the end. Still, we were really tight. But these days, all she seems to care about are clothes, boys, and skiing in Vermont with Vivian Butler and Daniel Reese and their whole crowd, The Tribe. It's weird when you used to totally know a person, then go to suddenly wondering if you ever actually did.

"Yeah, sure, we'll come," I say, glancing at Gellie to let her know she's included. Gellie doesn't notice, having immersed herself in a different rack of clothes, searching for the yellow T-shirt with the monkey on it, I guess.

Shawna narrows her eyes at me, but I look away. "Who are you going with?" I ask her, pretending to be interested in a blue velvet shirt.

"Derek," she says languidly. "And I know I'm going to regret it. He's going to think he's my *actual* boyfriend, when, in fact, he's just my place-saver boyfriend."

"What's that?" says Gellie, poking her head up.

This is why I am almost popular and Gellie is not.

"You know," says Shawna. "He'll do for now. He's on my level." Of popularity, is what she means. Shawna adds, "We hang out with the same kinds of people." She pulls out a pack of gum and offers me a stick. I shake my head. She puts it back in her back pocket without offering any to Gellie. She continues. "He'd be fine except for this thing he does when he gets nervous. He kind of clicks his teeth together in a really unnerving way." She pulls out her gum and imitates Derek clicking his teeth.

Last year Shawna's place-saver boyfriend was Timothy Snyder. He was just another version of Derek. But I know what she means. Having a boyfriend, any boyfriend, gives you at least ten points toward being popular.

"Also," Shawna continues, "he has this horrible laugh, like he's about to choke to death. So I try not to tell jokes when I'm around him. But he's cute. And he'll do for now, till someone better comes along."

"Ooh, like Martin Forrest!" squeals Essie. "I invited him to my party, Shawna, did I tell you?"

"Mmmm," says Shawna. "Hey, Randi. Call me tonight. We have a lot of catching up to do."

"OK," I say. "See ya." I decide the dark-blue velvet shirt would look great on Gellie. I find her in the back of the store pretending to be interested in socks. "Here. Try this on before we go."

☆ ☆ ☆

"How can you stand them?" hisses Gellie as we walk back to Yogi Dave's to get our bikes. "They're ridiculous and shallow."

"Hello! Being a teen model isn't exactly rocket science or the road to spiritual enlightenment."

Gellie doesn't say anything and pinches her mouth shut. I go on. "Give them a chance. They're . . . fun. And nice. Or at least, they can be. You've just got to get to know them, is all."

But I feel like I'm repeating the same line I say to Essie and Shawna about Gellie.

"Come with me to the party on Saturday," I say.

"No way. I don't need a pity invite."

"Just come. I promise it'll be fine."

"People are going to call me Peanut Butter And."

"No, they won't. And if they do, I'll beat them up."

"I won't have any friends there at all."

This is sad but kind of true. Gellie claims she doesn't like being with other people. Last year, after she found out that she was the only girl in our grade not invited to Shawna's spring fling, she said, "I don't want a social life. People let you down. But my career will never let me down, as long as I work hard. That's what my mom says."

"You'll have me," I say.

We are standing beside our bikes. Gellie has the bike lock in one hand and is bent over it, frozen as if she doesn't remember the combination. She looks up at me seriously.

"I'll think about it."

CHAPTER FOUR

Glow-in-the-Dark Plastic Angel

Gellie and I first figured out that we lived across the street from each other back in fifth grade. We were always the last two kids left at the car-pool circle. We bonded over our shared fantasy that our mothers were in a complex plot to abandon us. I can't remember all the details now, but it involved the CIA and microfilm.

To get to Gellie's house, I have to look both ways before crossing the road. Right, left. Right, left. Cross. It's my ritual.

I go into the house and head to Gellie's studio, a special room Mrs. Riddle set up for Gellie to practice being famous in. On the walls in the hallway there are poster-sized pictures of each of the three Riddle girls when they were much younger. Margie is the oldest, brown-haired and smart. She reads most of the time when she's home from college, or else she's out with Jeremy, who is not her boyfriend, just her friend who happens to be a boy. But most of the time she's away at college in Connecticut.

Barbara, the middle daughter, is tall and thin, blonde and athletic. She was president of the junior class at Clairman and captain of the varsity tennis team last year. I always wanted older sisters until I got to know Gellie's family. Gellie's sisters are amazing and talented. Margie got into Yale with the highest SAT score of anyone from our high school. When she was fourteen, she wrote an article for the Clairman *Observer* about a hazardous-waste dump in our area. That article got the dump closed down. And Barbara is ranked number one in her age group in tennis for the Southern New England region. The rule is, you can't be a Riddle without being amazing and talented. I'm glad I'm not a Riddle.

Then there's Gellie, tiny Gellie. In the poster of her as a little girl, she has a butterfly on her finger and is looking at it intently, with a serious expression on her face. Her eyes are as dark as watermelon seeds and shaped that way, too. She is wearing overalls and a hat made out of a folded newspaper. It sort of surprises me that Mrs. Riddle would hang a picture of Gellie looking like this. All the other pictures of Gellie are professional and look airbrushed.

When I open the door to her studio with mirrors for walls, Gellie is sitting on the floor with her back against the giant closet, which holds all of her auditioning clothes. She is playing her sister Margie's old guitar, a big jumbo with a neck so huge it's hard for me even to get my hands around it, and I'm a head taller than Gellie.

As soon as I come in, she hands the guitar to me. I start trying to play "Kiss Me on the Moon."

Gellie lies down on her back and folds her arms across her chest.

"That's a really great song," she says. "I wish I could write songs."

"Me, too," I say. And the moment suddenly appears, like a big translucent bubble, the kind Glinda the Good Witch was inside in *The Wizard of Oz*. I can practically hear Glinda whisper, "Ask her. Tell her. Now's the time." I feel sick to my stomach, but I finally say it.

"I've been thinking," I begin, "that maybe it would be fun if you and I . . . actually tried to . . . I mean . . . what if we tried to be a rock band?"

Gellie just looks at me from her position on her back. "OK," she says. "That sounds fun."

I can't believe it was this easy.

"It's not that easy," I say, frowning. "Making music for a living is the hardest thing you can ever do. It takes time and talent and practice and you get turned down a lot and . . ."

"Whoa!" says Gellie, sitting up. "I never said anything

35

about making a living! We're thirteen years old. Can't we just kind of play guitar and sing together?"

I stop, my mouth open. I want the idea of being in a band to be a bigger deal for her. I want it to be a sacrifice. Maybe that's asking too much.

"Yeah, I mean. That's cool." And I go back to strumming the guitar. We sing the first couple of verses again. Then we come to the chorus, and I still can't play those stupid barre chords.

"I think I know them," says Gellie, reaching for the guitar. And she plays the chorus, barre chords and all.

"How did you do that?" I sputter.

"Dunno," says Gellie. "I've been playing this guitar a lot. My mom sends me in here to practice all the time. She says I have to practice my *walk*. Can you believe that? You just kind of wiggle your hips and walk. What's there to practice? But my mom says I need to do it like a pro, and she makes me practice for an hour a day. About three months ago, I started playing this guitar instead, but I've had to do it quietly so my mom wouldn't hear me. Margie has all these old songbooks, so I've been kind of teaching myself." And she shows me her stash of guitar books in the back of the closet. Gellie knows a lot of songs already, so we play through a bunch. Mostly Gellie sings lead and I sing harmony but sometimes the opposite. I think we sound great together.

"We need a name," I say breathlessly. "And we need to be really disciplined about practicing. Dad says the difference between a musician and someone who just plays for fun is the amount of time you practice."

Gellie is looking down at the guitar, picking at the frets with her fingernail. She doesn't say anything for a few seconds.

"I'm not sure it's a good idea for me to tell my mom about this," she says finally.

"Why not?"

"She doesn't like me to have what she calls distractions," Gellie explains. "In case some big job comes up for me and I have to go."

"Oh," I say. "OK, Your Goddessness."

Gellie glares at me. I glare back. I don't want to be Gellie's Plan B. I want to be Plan A. But I'm not going to convince her by glaring. So I take my fingers and pull my eyebrows and the corners of my mouth up and give her a big hilarious smile.

Gellie cracks up, leaning backward into her open closet, filled with unfolded clothes. "Maybe I want some distractions. What Mom doesn't know won't hurt her."

Then her voice changes.

"Can I ask you a question?" Gellie says to the ceiling.

"Uh-huh," I say. I pick at the guitar strings, tuning it the way my father taught me.

"When you get your period . . . ," Gellie hesitates. "Is it . . . like . . . *really* bloody?"

I think about it. I got my period in the beginning of sixth grade. Three years ago.

"I think my first period was more like a rust stain," I say.

Gellie props herself up on her elbows. "Then I think maybe I got my period," she says.

"When?" I say, trying not to look as amazed as I feel. I know Gellie is touchy about her status as Last Girl on the Planet Earth to Menstruate.

"Two days ago. I already stopped bleeding. If that's what you want to call it. So I actually don't know. Maybe it was nothing."

I don't say anything. I don't want to ask about the details. Of course, when I got my period, my mom was all, "Oh, HONEY! You're a woman now!" and took me out to dinner. But not before she made me show her the bloody underpants. She practically wanted to have them framed. Or bronzed. But that's my mother. It's not the way they do things at the Riddle house.

Finally, the quiet makes me nervous enough to say, "Did you tell your mom?" I don't bother to ask if she'd told Margie or Barbara. They'd be the last people Gellie would talk to about something like this.

Gellie shakes her head no.

"We can go to my house," I quickly say. "Mom was supposed to pick up some pads on her way home today. Mom and I both get our periods at the same time now. We call our period 'Fred.' Fred should be coming next week. Mom says we're so regular, you could set an egg timer by us, so to speak."

"Maybe we can get a ride into town," says Gellie. "I kind of want to get a soda and a magazine. I'll buy my first rags. I should have my own stash."

Only Gellie would call sanitary napkins rags. She probably got that from Margie. From now on, I will, too. It's retro.

Then Gellie dives into the closet.

"Don't come in here!" she calls over her shoulder. "It's a disgusting mess."

She reemerges with a little plastic angel, sort of greenish, the kind you're supposed to put on a computer for good luck or that taxi drivers stick on their dashboards.

"This will be our guardian angel," she intones. "Our glow-in-the-dark plastic angel, who will gently guide us on our rock-and-roll path." And she winds up the crank on the back so its wings move mechanically up and down, making a soft little buzz. She shines a flashlight on the angel for a long moment and then turns out the lights in her studio. The angel glows for five minutes and then disappears in the darkness.

Mrs. Riddle is sitting at the kitchen table, staring at a scrapbook she made of Gellie's career. She'd stenciled on the front of it MY BEAUTIFUL GIRL. She's beautiful herself. She is tall, freckled, and has the kind of spirit that makes you want her to like you. Gellie says she used to be a star on Broadway. Her coarse, thick blond hair (dyed, Mom told me and Gellie confirmed) floats just below her shoulders, and she wears it pulled back in a barrette most of the time. Not a thin barrette but one of those big thick ones. She beams at us when we come into the kitchen.

"Lovey," she says, wrinkling her nose at Gellie. "How's my baby girl?" Margie and Barbara might be amazing and talented, but Gellie is definitely her mother's favorite.

"Fine," says Gellie. "Mom, will you take us to the Clairman Mall?"

"Ask one of your sisters," says Mrs. Riddle, sorting through some photos.

"Hi, Mrs. Riddle," I say, pulling up a stool. She smiles at me with her lips closed.

"How's your mother, Randi?" she asks. She always asks how Mom is, never Dad.

"Fine," I say. "She's just got her license to start practicing acupuncture."

"Uh-huh," she says. "Does she have a . . . I mean, does she go work in a . . . *hospital* for that?"

"No," I say. "She can work out of our house. She's even got her own clients now."

"Well, that must be very fulfilling for her," says Mrs. Riddle. She pulls out a couple of Gellie's modeling shots. "I'm sending off a new press kit to this agency I read about online. They specialize in child artists who are ready for a new stage." She raises her eyebrows. "Sounds perfect for us, doesn't it?"

"I guess," says Gellie.

Barbara comes downstairs swinging her car keys on her right finger.

"Will you drive us to the mall, Barbara?" says Gellie.

"No," says Barbara.

"Barbara, take the girls," Mrs. Riddle says. "I have work to do here."

Barbara looks over her mother's shoulder at Gellie's scrapbook and rolls her eyes. "Can't they go outside and play?"

This is the thing about coming over here. Everyone treats Gellie like she's a baby, especially Barbara. It drives me crazy, though I get a sort of secret pleasure from hanging out with Gellie, as though I'm on vacation from being older. When I'm with Shawna and Essie, I have to act 100 percent cool. With Gellie, I can be all sorts of things.

Margie comes up from the basement with Jeremy. Jeremy wears all black, even in the summer. Margie refuses to shave her armpits or legs, even though Mrs. Riddle is always giving her lectures about the importance of good grooming. Margie and Jeremy don't fit in, in Clairman, either. Margie introduced Gellie to David Bowie and the B-52s and all these great bands from the 1980s. She's been trying to indoctrinate Gellie with anti-Clairman rhetoric since Gellie was born. I regard Margie as an untrustworthy ally.

"Margie, will you drive us to the mall?" Gellie asks.

Jeremy laughs. Margie does, too. "Are you kidding?" she says. "It's been two years since I set foot in that morass of rampant craving and greed. I'd rather have a chemical peel."

"What's so bad about it?" says Gellie.

"It's part of the bourgeois *conspiracy*?" says Jeremy.

"Haven't you noticed that whenever you go there, you feel so rotten about yourself and the things you don't have that you're compelled to spend all your disposable income on things you don't need, all in order to feel socially *acceptable*?" Margie says. *"Gaw!"*

"Gellie, you can go to the mall later this week," Mrs. Riddle says. "You need to get a haircut for the Thursday photo shoot. And the two of us need to sit down and go through your portfolio. There are a lot of outdated shots and clippings in here."

I whisper to Gellie, "Let's go to my house."

As we're heading out the door, Mrs. Riddle calls after us, "And don't forget that audition for the hair commercial."

Back in my room I pick up the guitar and play a few chords. I spent all day figuring them out. They're really tricky, but after you play something two million times for your cat, you sort of get it.

Kiss me on the moon,
Wrap me in the stars,
Tell me you'll be coming home soon,
Show me who you are.

Gellie says, "Wow. Those are hard chords." And she starts to sing along. I'm always singing Dad's song so she knows it really well. I switch to a low harmony.

Circle round the sun,
Keep me company,
Tell me I'm the only one
That you want to see.

Gellie's voice becomes more pointed, now that I've joined her. We lock eyes and both of us get louder on the bridge.

You tell me we're not there yet
But someday we might be.
The closer that I let you get
The farther I can see.

Don't let me forget,
Don't let me assume.
Promise what we haven't done yet,
Kiss me on the moon.

Then we repeat softly,

Promise what we haven't done yet,
Kiss me on the moon.

The room holds the echo of the last notes for half a minute after we finish.

"We sound really good together," Gellie says. "This is going to be great, you and me being in a band."

"If you ever even have time to see me again," I grumble. "After that list your mom laid down just now, I'll be surprised if I get to sing with you before school starts."

"Eh," says Gellie. "Relax. We'll sing together. We're meant to. Isn't it obvious?"

I think so, but I don't say anything.

"Want to come with me to the mall to get my hair cut?"

"Maybe." I feel so almost happy. Singing with Gellie just now was magical. I want to go back where our voices made that amazing sound together.

But this is all too easy. I don't think Gellie gets it that she can't be a supermodel child star with her mother jumping up and down alongside her *and* be in a band with me. And there's this third thing I want from Gellie. I just want her to be my friend, to hang out with me, to be a normal kid who goes to parties, like normal kids do. Who — dare I say it? — tries to be popular like any normal kid would try to be.

"I'll tell you what," I say. "I'll make a deal with you. I'll go to the mall to watch you get your hair cut if you'll go with me to Essie's party."

Gellie looks at me as if I've just asked her to strip naked and dance on her roof. "I don't know. I have something to do on Sunday morning."

"What?" I say.

"Well, mostly running around with Mom doing errands. I have to get ready for next week's audition in Boston."

"Sounds glam, Your Goddessness," I say, unenthusiastically.

"I wish," says Gellie. "But it's just a lot of sitting around waiting for people to pay attention to you. My mom says it'll lead to bigger things."

"Come on," I wheedle. "Just come to the party. We can tell everyone we're in a band together."

"I'll think about it," says Gellie, "but I need to get home for dinner now."

"Wait two seconds," I say, and duck into my bathroom. I pull a handful of pads from the basket I keep behind the toilet and wrap them up in a dirty T-shirt from the hamper. "Here," I say casually, handing the bundle to Gellie. "For next month."

"Thanks," mumbles Gellie.

She leaves the house and goes to the edge of the road. She looks both ways before crossing.

CHAPTER FIVE

Essie's Party

Saturday night, Gellie and I go to Essie's party. Gellie has on the blue velvet shirt over the yellow monkey tee that we bought in Jintucket. And a new haircut. Only not at the place Mrs. Riddle usually takes her to. That's because Mrs. Riddle wasn't there. Margie said she'd take us to Jintucket but refused to take us to the mall. As a result, Gellie got her hair cut by Patrick at Panacea.

Gellie's new haircut looks amazing. It's all piecey, in soft layers around her face, shoulder length. It cuts away from her cheeks and gives her an elflike look. Her huge eyes look even bigger, and her high forehead is framed by cute little bangs.

Of course, her mother almost disowned her.

"It'll take years to grow that back! Years, young lady!" she'd shouted. "Why do young people insist upon mutilating themselves?" She was so furious about the hair, she didn't even notice the yellow T-shirt.

Gellie had been miserable all afternoon. "I wish I'd never cut it," she moaned.

"Why?" I'd said. "Don't you like your hair now?"

"Yeah," she'd admitted, wiping her nose. "I really do. But my mom hates it."

"So?" I'd said. "It's not her hair."

Gellie had looked at me doubtfully, as if she weren't so sure.

☆ ☆ ☆

Essie greets us at the door. Her mother and father are rushing around in black-tie attire, getting last-minute things done before they leave for their event. Essie's brother, Paul, and his girlfriend, Francie, are chaperoning, but we all know what that means. It means they'll be up in Paul's room making out all night.

Essie's eyes open wide when she sees Gellie. I'm afraid she's going to kill me for bringing Gellie, but instead she gushes.

"Gellie, I love your hair!" She reaches over and pulls at the ends. "Adorable!"

Gellie smiles and shakes her hair, looking for a second like the model I saw on the runway. But then she says, "My mom practically killed me. I've been so upset about it all day long. I've never gone to get my hair cut without her, and now she'll probably never let me again."

Essie looks at her and opens her mouth. Then she looks at me as if to say, "What a freak!" She may as well have said it. Gellie shuts up and looks panicked.

The Tribe is here. Daniel Reese, Vivian Butler, Lloyd Proctor, Derek Jacobs, Martin Forrest, Shawna Gilbert, and Essie, of course. They are beautiful and dressed as if they didn't think at all about what they were going to wear, though I know every single one of them probably spent an hour getting the "whatever" look just right. I scan the room for someone who might give Gellie a chance.

"Well, if it isn't Angela Riddle," says a voice coming from the music room. A short boy with big brown eyes approaches us, the one and only Terry Duganton. Unfortunately, he's wearing a Hawaiian shirt.

"Hi, Duge," I say.

"Randi," he nods cordially. But he really is not at all interested in me. "I saw on the local news that you won the Are You a Goddess contest, Angela. Kudos!"

"Thanks," murmurs Gellie.

"It's really cool that you're a model," Essie says, trying to be a good hostess. "I always . . . wondered what that would be like."

"Actually, sometimes modeling's not all that great," Gellie says too loudly. "Like when they're doing your makeup for a TV commercial. They talk about you like you're not there. They say things like, 'Oh, God, the eyes look like a thirty-five-year-old's. What are we going to do about the eyes?' Like my eyes don't even belong to me. Or they'll kind of pick up my hair and hold it out and say, '*This* is a hairstyle? What do we *call* this thing?'"

"Ugh!" I say. "You're totally just a piece of meat to them!"

"Oh, but they can be really sweet, too," Gellie quickly adds. "I mean, this one producer always sends me holiday cards and birthday cards and stuff like that. She even knows what my favorite color is."

"So do I," says Duge, all googly-eyed. "It's blue."

We drift to the back room, which Essie has outfitted with a black light and lava lamps. Someone brought a bottle of vodka, and one by one Duge lets us have a swig; he's sort of policing the situation from the recliner. I don't like alcohol, but I put my mouth to the bottle and pretend to drink. I'm taking my third fake swig when Duge grabs the bottle from me and shoves it back under the cushion of the chair.

"You kids call on the cell phone if you need us," says Essie's mother, poking her head in. She's wearing a short black dress and a gold necklace, and her chin-length dark hair is pulled neatly behind her ears.

"Bye, Mom," sings Essie. Half of our class is here tonight and at least a third of the ninth graders, too. Outside on the back porch, they light up cigarettes as soon as they hear the Reynolds' car drive away.

I lead Gellie over to the pool table, which Essie's mother has covered with a white cloth and big bottles of orange soda, Coke, and Sprite, and huge bowls of Cheetos, pretzels, and M&Ms. Shawna and Vivian make room for us, and Essie follows with refills. Shawna is wearing a crocheted top, low-slung suede pants, and a bronze medallion that hangs down to just above her navel. Her clothes are all gold colored and her hair is a shiny dark brown. She looks like she stepped out of a fashion magazine. It's funny how Gellie actually *is* a model but doesn't seem like one, and Shawna isn't but does.

"What do you guys think," I say, pouring myself an orange soda. "I'm pretty sure Duge likes Gellie. Don't you think they should go out?"

"He's certainly available," Vivian Butler says and shrugs.

"He has sweaty palms," Essie says, making a face.

"So?" I say. "That's not what's important."

"He's a *bando*," says Vivian through a mouthful of M&Ms.

Bandos are people in marching band. OK, so they are kind of dorky. Plus, there's something about being in marching band that makes a person a target. Maybe the fake enthusiasm. Or something about the way they all turn the same way together on the football field.

Shawna turns her regal head elegantly in Gellie's direction and focuses on her.

"Not everyone can have whatever guy they want," she says. "At some point, you have to just say yes to the guy who likes you."

"He hasn't asked me anything yet," says Gellie, pretending not to care that Shawna insulted her.

"He's a really good musician," I persist. "He can play any instrument there is, except the guitar. I think he's probably the most talented musician in the whole school. It's just that he likes classical and jazz, and not so much pop. Besides, I'd call him an emo more than a bando."

"What's an emo?" says Gellie.

"You know," I say. "Into emotional music. Serious stuff."

Gellie looks at me and rolls her eyes. I look to Shawna and Essie for support. Shawna has already left us, at least in spirit. Her head has turned in the same direction as her outside foot, and she's gazing over at a group of upper-school students who have just come in. I want to help Gellie, but it looks like this discussion is over for now.

I go into the back room and find Duge playing a guitar.

"I thought you couldn't play guitar," I say.

"I can't," he says as he practically plays a symphony all over the neck.

"What's that? Computer code?" I crack.

Duge just shrugs. "I don't know what I'm doing, really. Just messing around. I figured it had to be something like the violin." And he continues to play something fast and amazing on the guitar, using just one finger.

"That's good messing," I say.

"It's just math. I'd give anything to be able to sing. Here." And he hands me the guitar. I play "Kiss Me on the

Moon" and sing a little bit, and then I hear a voice behind me, singing along. It's Gellie. I switch to the harmony and Gellie takes the melody.

Essie comes in and listens. When we're done, she claps, looking a little shocked. "Oh, my God," she says. "That was, like, incredible!"

"Sing another," urges Duge, sitting at Gellie's feet. "You guys are great. You should call yourselves something and start a band."

I look at Gellie. She is beaming. "We *are* a band," she tells him.

"Right on," says Duge. His voice is just changing, so "right" is high and "on" is low.

This is good. Duge is in on Tribe gossip. Duge will tell everyone.

"What's your band called?" he says.

"Plastic Angel," says Gellie confidently, as if we've been called this forever. It's not a bad name. It'll do till we think of something brilliant.

"I think we should call the band 'The Plastic Angels' instead of 'Plastic Angel,'" I say. "All the best bands have a 'the' in front of their name. The Beatles. The Rolling Stones. The Who."

"No," says Gellie. "It's got to be Plastic Angel. Like Plastic Ono Band. Besides. *We're* not the plastic angels. It's the *metaphor* of the plastic angel."

Duge says, "Isn't it *The* Plastic Ono Band?"

"PLASTIC ANGEL," Gellie says emphatically, but she

is grinning. It's as though someone turned a light on inside her. She glows. I like it so much more than when she wears makeup.

Martin Forrest has ambled over to the coffee table. I realize he's been staring at me in this way that I've never been stared at by a boy. It's as though I'm someone else, someone I don't know, but he does. It's scary and really exciting at the same time. I keep catching his glance and smiling at him. When I do that, he smiles back, like we're playing catch.

Shawna comes in from outside with Lloyd, a tenth grader with blond hair and a dimple in his chin. He's the head lifeguard at the Clairman YMCA. Martin looks up at her, and I see him try to give her the same look he's been giving me all night. But Shawna ignores him. Something else is on her mind. Us. Singing. She heard.

"Kumbaya ya ya, kumbaya," she sings loudly, mocking us. "Can we have some real music, please?"

So Essie hurries to get up, turns down the lights, and turns on the stereo, blasting techno music.

Soon everyone is dancing, and the room gets really hot. Over on the couches, couples are entwined, kissing and writhing and sweating — and I can't help but stare at them through the haze in the room. I don't want anyone to see me looking. But then I see Martin watching me, and I see him dancing over. He grabs me and pulls me close to him, and I can feel all of him against me. The music pounds away and suddenly we're lost in our own groove.

We dance for what seems like hours. Then Martin puts his hand on my chin and turns my face toward him. Is he going to kiss me? I've never been kissed before. I think I want to. I know I want to. Now my heart starts pounding so hard, I'm afraid he'll feel it. Martin has straight dark hair and gray eyes the color of iron. He moves as though he never needs to think about where his body ought to go. It just goes. I close my eyes and he moves in. I can't believe this is about to happen!

Then I feel someone tap my shoulder. It's Gellie.

"My mom's here," she announces.

"Already?" I shout over the music. My mother drove us here, and Mrs. Riddle is our ride home, but I never expected her to come so early. I check my watch. It's only ten-fifteen.

"I have a ton of stuff to do tomorrow, remember?" Gellie shouts back.

"My mom can give you a ride later," Martin says to me. I consider the drive back to my house, sitting in the back-seat next to Martin.

"Great!" I shout. "OK." I turn to Gellie. She looks really hurt and stands next to me, hovering.

"Fine," she says finally. "See ya."

"Bye," I call gaily.

Shawna is dancing with Lloyd and ignoring Derek, her place-saver boyfriend. Martin keeps glancing over at her, but she and Lloyd start slow dancing, even though the music seems to get louder and faster with a thumping bass.

Martin says something I can't hear.

"What?"

"I said, do you want to go outside and get some air?"

"Yeah, sure," I say. Martin sprays Binaca in his mouth cockily and saunters out, leading me by the hand. I feel like everyone's watching as we walk out.

We go out to the back porch. There's another couple making out on the swing. Martin takes my hand and pulls me after him. We go over to Essie's trampoline, in the corner of the backyard, under a gigantic pine tree. The moon is rising, almost three-quarters full and kind of blurry from the humidity. The mosquitoes are out full force. I slap one on my upper arm. Martin lifts me up and tosses me onto the trampoline as if I weigh nothing. Then he jumps up after me. We bounce for a few minutes, giggling and trying to knock each other over. When the bouncing stops, he crawls across and kisses me hard on the mouth. It happens so fast and it's over so fast that I can't believe it actually happened. It is big and wet and sloppy and . . . well, mouthy. I can't help but think of Aunt Izzie's dog, Kramer. Also, I can't tell if it's the Binaca or what, but he tastes like medicine.

"I always thought you had a crush on Shawna," I murmur after the kiss.

"Yeah," he says. "So what? Is she here?"

Martin starts to put his hand under my tank top, and I pull away. I wanted him to touch me but not like this, not this fast. My mind races for a way out.

"I'm getting eaten alive," I say. "Let's go back in."

He sighs dramatically and gets down off the trampoline.

☆ ☆ ☆

Back inside, Shawna is sitting on the couch, tucked under the arm of Lloyd the Lifesaver.

"Have fun?" she smirks at us.

"Oh, yeah," I say. "Totally."

Martin goes over to a group of his friends and swaggers around with them. I just got kissed for the first time. Soon, his mother will come and we will sit next to each other for the ride home. I thought I'd want that. But the idea of another slobbery kiss from Martin is so not what I want. Suddenly, the image of Gellie's face looms in front of me. I should have gone home with her. Now that I'm back inside, in the light, I feel this knot in my stomach, two parts guilt, two parts sad, one part disappointment.

CHAPTER SIX

cute, Skinny Knees

What's for breakfast?" I say.

"Oatmeal," Mom replies. She's paying bills at the kitchen table. Her coffee is steaming next to her, but she hasn't taken a sip. It's going to get cold. So's the oatmeal on the stove. I get up and stir it.

As usual, Mom is worried about money. Three of her five acupuncture clients didn't come this week. Her official policy is to charge them if they cancel less than twenty-four hours before their scheduled appointment, but she never does.

"When you're starting out like I am, you can't afford to

be a hard-ass," she says. "Your father says I wouldn't have this problem if we lived across the river, because here people think of acupuncture as voodoo, so if they miss an appointment, they just don't bother to pay." She closes her eyes and rubs them with the palms of her hands. Dad's away again, this time in the Midwest. There are Xs on the calendar where Mom and I cross out the days until he comes home. She forgot to X out yesterday, so I do.

In past summers, I'd be sitting in the backseat of our old VW van. We'd start out at ten in the morning and drive all day to the next gig, Dad at the wheel, Mom in the front seat with her feet up on the dashboard. She used to wear her hair long, pulled behind her ears. They'd play Beatles tapes on the car stereo. One summer the tape player broke, and we never got around to getting it fixed. So we listened to the radio instead, playing Name That Tune. Whoever guessed the song first got to decide where we went for dinner. Dad always won, but he always let Mom choose.

Once, Mom wore a blue-and-green striped sleeveless T-shirt and a ribbon in her hair. I remember thinking how young she looked, realizing for the first time that my mother was pretty. She wasn't the kind who tried to be.

Mom's hair is shoulder length now, like all moms' hair seems to be. I put my hand on her mug. It's barely lukewarm. She's never going to drink it.

The phone rings. "Finally," says Mom, picking up the receiver on the table with one hand. She gets my breakfast off the stove with the other hand and plunks it down in front of me. "How was the turnout?" she asks into the phone.

I am dying to pick up the extension on the kitchen wall, but Mom hates it when I do that because then she can't hear Dad as well and my voice sounds super loud in her ear. Of course, hers does in mine, too, but I don't mind.

"Uh-huh. Oh. Well. It's summertime. People like to barbecue and don't want to be indoors." And she motions to me to start eating. I shake my head. She glares at me and says, "Your daughter won't eat until after she's talked to you," and hands me the phone.

"Hi, Dad," I say.

"Do you know what would be the first foreign soil you'd hit if you were standing in downtown Detroit and started walking south?" he asks. He sounds far away and sleepy.

"Mexico?" I say.

"Nope."

I take the phone into the living room and twirl the globe around fast. "Brazil?"

"Nope. One more guess." This time I stop the twirling globe and look closely at the tiny little lakes around the state of Michigan. I can hear noises at the other end of the phone; it sounds like a low roar, or the ocean. I squint and concentrate.

"Windsor, Ontario," I declare.

"Way to go!" says Dad. "Sweetheart, put your mother back on."

Slowly I get up and shuffle back to the kitchen and hand

Mom the phone. "Just a minute," she says into the mouth-piece. "Randi, eat your breakfast." She takes the phone into the bedroom with her. I eat my oatmeal, one sticky spoonful at a time. I hear my mother raise her voice from behind her closed door. I want to tell Mom that Gellie got her hair cut. I want to tell Dad how Gellie and I sang at the party last night.

Mom comes back in with an inscrutable look on her face and gives me the phone again. This time, Dad seems to be in a better mood, or at least he's good at faking it.

"So, Glory girl, I talked to John. You're all set at Real Tunes. He can't pay you, but the experience will be valu-able in itself. Go over there today, and he'll figure out what you can do for him."

Suddenly, the oatmeal tastes just fine. In fact, it's the best oatmeal Mom's ever made me. I clean my plate faster than I ever have, kiss her good-bye, run to the garage, and jump on my bike.

Across the street, Gellie's getting into her car with her mother. She totally saw me coming out of the house, but she pretends not to. I feel another stab of guilt for staying at the party last night instead of going home with her. I want to tell her about kissing Martin, but I'm not sure what she'll think.

"Hey," I say, biking a slow circle around their silver Volvo.

"Oh, hi," Gellie says, halfway in the car, halfway out. "How was the rest of the party?"

I shrug. "Fine. You didn't miss much."

"No?"

"Nope."

But Gellie looks at me like I've completely betrayed her, gives me one long glare, then turns her head and looks straight out the front. "It's good I left," she says. "I have a full day ahead of me."

"That's for sure, little star," chirps Mrs. Riddle. "First we're going to straighten out this awful hairdo. Randi, can you believe the job they did on her at that butchery in Jintucket? No one over on that side of the river knows a thing about hair. I'm going to have Marie do it at Salon 34. I'm thinking hair extensions, Gel. What do you think?"

Gellie shrugs. "Whatever."

"And then we need to practice your dialogue for the hair-product commercial . . . ," Mrs. Riddle continues, pulling out her big legal notepad — Gellie's never-ending To Do list.

"See you," I say, backing up on my bike. "I have to go to Real Tunes."

"Have fun," says Gellie, not looking at me.

"You, too," I say.

I bike through downtown Clairman on my way to Jintucket. The decorations are still up from the Founders' Day parade, the annual event where Clairmanites all get together to celebrate the day the Puritans kicked out the

Indians and started making their teenage daughters' lives miserable.

As soon as I cross the Jintucket River, I can feel my shoulders loosen up. It's the kind of town where you just feel comfortable in whatever body you happen to be in and whatever clothes you happen to have draped onto it.

I park my bike in front of Real Tunes and put my hand on the front door. Then I stop, realizing the enormity of the situation. This is my first actual day of work! I have a job!

John opens the door before I can, and I feel stupid for standing there doing nothing.

"Brilliant," he says, motioning me in frantically. "There are twenty boxes of the new Dave Matthews CD, and his record company just decided to sell them for $13.99 instead of $15.99. Can you resticker them? Here." He hands me a roll of stickers that say $13.99 and points me to the back room, where all the brown shoe-box-size boxes of CDs are kept. They all look exactly alike.

"Labels," John says, reading my thoughts and pointing at the bottom of each box. And he goes to the back room to meet the delivery truck. Four new guitars arrive in big cardboard boxes, and John hangs each one of them on the guitar wall, carefully and lovingly.

I spend my first morning at Real Tunes going through five hundred Dave Matthews CDs. I make a game out of putting the sticker in the very best place on the cover so the important words and pictures still show. I have to hide a flower, but that doesn't seem so bad. John spends the morning selling guitars. By lunchtime, he's already sold half the new ones and one of the older ones.

"Crackerjack day," John says. "I'm off to Tia Maria's. D'you want some takeaway?"

I shake my head. In my rush this morning, I forgot to pack a lunch, but as usual, I'm broke.

"Right, then." But he comes back two minutes later.

"You know, Randi, I can't legally pay you. So, for as long as you work here, lunch is on me."

He hands me a takeout menu, and I try to focus on it, but it takes me a million years to decide what to get because I'm so nervous.

"California Burrito," I say finally. "With roasted corn chipotle salsa."

"Excellent choice," says John, smiling.

☆ ☆ ☆

We eat our burritos out in front of the shop at the little picnic table he's set up. I sit on a chair while he leans against the low wall that has flower beds built into it. I'm trying not to stare at him, but every time he moves, I want to watch exactly how he does what he does. It's really hard to eat the burrito. It seems huge and intolerably messy.

He licks his fingers when his burrito is gone. In his adorable British accent, he says, "Like I said, I can't legally pay you. And I've been trying to figure out how to make this worth your while."

I want to say I'd work for free. I want to say I'd pay him

to let me hang out with him all day. Instead, I just mumble, "Whatever you think."

"Well," he says, crumpling up the wrapper. "Your dad did mention that you are an aspiring guitar player. And that he isn't going to be around much this summer, and so he can't teach you as often as he'd like to. And I play a little. So I was thinking, maybe I could pay you in guitar lessons. After work every day, we could go through songs together. How's that? I mean, I'm nowhere near as talented as your dad. But I fiddle around a bit."

Dad's not going to teach me anymore? After only a few lessons? I think about the card he gave me for Christmas: GOOD FOR FIVE GUITAR LESSONS. I didn't think he literally meant only five lessons. I expected him to teach me until I was done learning.

But then I think about all the extra time I'd get to stare at John's cute little skinny knees if he were my teacher.

"Sure," I say, very cool. "You know, I have my own band."

"Really now?" says John. "Got to start a bin for you, eh? What're you called, then?"

"Plastic Angel," I say. "Me and my friend, Gellie, actually. We don't have a record yet. But we're working on it."

John smiles. "I'll start a bin for you, anyway. It'll be empty, but that will be intriguing. People will say, 'When are you ever going to get this record in?' And I'll say it's extremely rare and hard to find. Then when you and your friend Jellybean actually do put a CD out, people will snatch it up in a jiffy."

I can't even respond to this. This is so much better than getting paid. I manage to squeak out, "That's really . . . that would be cool."

John jumps up. "Oh! And I wanted you to check out this hip band I can't stop listening to. You'll love them."

He goes into the store and comes back outside with a record by a band called The Big Idea. The cover has a photo of a purple house with green shutters.

"Local band," says John. "But they just got signed to a major label. They're going to be huge. And they're massively prolific. This is their third record. All their CDs have a minimum of eighteen songs. I think all of their members must write."

"Uh . . . huh," I say.

"Give it a listen," says John.

CHAPTER SEVEN

Nothing More Beautiful Than a Girl in Love

When I get home that afternoon, I put the Big Idea CD in my boom box. I know right away that this is my kind of music. Two women's voices sing together, and the songs are strong and warm.

I open the cover of the CD booklet and stare at the picture of the people in the band. Two women: one with long dark hair in braids and one with a round face and curly blonde hair. Two men: a tall skinny man with black curls and one with a goatee and glasses.

The phone rings. It's Gellie. Before I can tell her about The Big Idea, she says breathlessly, "Come over right away! I think I just wrote my first song."

☆ ☆ ☆

Gellie is sitting cross-legged on her studio floor. Her hair has extensions now. It looks weird and fake. I decide not to mention it, and instead focus on her open notebook. The page is covered with her sparkly gel-pen handwriting.

"Listen to this," she says.

The town where everything is clean
But nothing is the way it seems.
We all need a little someplace else now and then,
We can't change the season.

I'm walking by St. Arthur's home,
He won't come out, he's all alone.
We all need somebody's hand to hold now and then,
We all need a reason.

The tune is swinging, familiar. I'm sure I've never heard it before, but I could sing it right away. Gellie fingers Margie's guitar with three chords — G, D, and E-minor. The easiest chords in the world. And yet, she's written a song that doesn't sound easy. It sounds like a song you'd hear on the radio. Now she sings the chorus, and her clear voice soars up and touches high notes easily.

In Clairman Town, Clairman Town,
Everybody walks with their head bowed down,

But I'll stand up straight, stand up tall,
And look you in the eye.

I saw you talk behind my back,
I'm ready for your next attack.
We all have our little scars to hide, I don't mind,
That's what makes me stronger.
You think you know me inside out,
You know what I am all about.
I can act like I'm as clean as you, time will tell
Who can hold out longer.

"That's really good," I say. Instinctively, I'm already tinkering with it. I take the notebook from her and study the words. "What if you start it with 'I live where everything is clean' instead of 'The town where everything is clean.'"

Gellie nods. "Yeah. That's better. What else?"

"Well," I hesitate. "How about instead of saying 'he's all alone' about St. Arthur, you say 'on the phone'? That's not so cliché."

Gellie considers.

"Actually," I continue, emboldened, "get rid of St. Arthur. That's so Dylan wannabe. Why don't you make it about —" I catch myself before I say "Shawna and Essie" because I suddenly realize she's writing about how mean they can be to her. Instead, I say, "The later verse. Make it about that person."

"Hmm," says Gellie. She scribbles for a second and then

pauses. Her eyes darken her face when she concentrates like this, and I watch the way the hairs on her eyebrows extend almost to her ears. For such a tiny person, she has gigantic eyebrows.

"How about this," Gellie says suddenly, picking her guitar back up. I stop spacing out and listen. She sings:

You told me I could count on you,
When times were tough you'd see me through.
We all need somebody's hand to hold now and then,
We all need a reason.

"Yeah." I nod. "Yeah. Much better." This isn't just about Shawna and Essie. I'm the one who told her she could count on me. I let her down when I didn't leave the party with her.

We are sitting on the floor of her studio. My legs make a V. Hers are crossed, and she is hunched over the guitar, its big curve in her lap. She picks at the strings softly, one at a time.

"Randi," she says finally. "Try singing along." And she turns the sheet of paper around so I can see the words. First, I try to sing a part that's higher than hers, but then I find a really cool lower part. We sing it over and over until I get it to ring with her voice every time. By now I've memorized the words.

"OK," I say. "This is really good."

Gellie's smiling to the guitar on her lap. "I think today marks the day we are officially a band."

"I think so, too."

"I think we need a ritual to commemorate the event." And Gellie gets the plastic angel out of the little box in the guitar case and places it on the floor. She seems to have forgiven me, if not forgotten about the other night. Neither of us mentions Essie's party. I still want to tell her about Martin — but not now.

I wind up the glow-in-the-dark plastic angel. As we watch it flap its mechanical wings back and forth, I say, "My aunt Izzie is coming over for dinner tomorrow. Want to come, too? Dad's going to be back from his tour."

Aunt Izzie is ten years older than my dad, and she lives in an apartment in a vine-covered house in Jintucket's Old Town, off Canal Street. She lives here about half the year, and the other half in Taos, New Mexico. She gets sick of the hustle and bustle of the Northeast and needs to go clear her head in the desert. But then she says she gets tired of the dryness of the Southwest and needs to hydrate. "Like a plant," she says.

She's an artist. She's even had a few exhibitions. When I come over, she takes me to her studio and lets me make my own statues out of clay. A huge window in her workroom faces the Jintucket River. Last summer when Mom was taking a one-week training course to get certified as an acupuncturist and Dad was on the road, I stayed with Aunt Izzie. It rained all week, but I didn't mind. She and I worked all day long in her studio and listened to her dusty old boom box. Every time a really good song came on, Aunt Izzie made me stop whatever I was doing and we'd scream the lyrics at the top of our lungs.

Mom and Dad have been fighting ever since Dad got back late last night. Not fighting, exactly. Just not really talking to each other. Right before Gellie got here, I heard a door slam and Mom came out of the bedroom with red eyes. She hates it when I ask her what's wrong, so I just try to be nice to her.

"Tell Gellie the story about the time you lived with Aunt Izzie," I say as the three of us make Mom's specialty, paella, for dinner. I'm shelling the shrimp, and I like the feeling of their papery skins. Gellie is a vegetarian and refuses even to touch them. She's helping Mom chop peppers and onions.

"Oh, you know," says Mom, distracted, and I'm afraid the story will get lost in the paella. Then she starts to tell it.

"I'd left Ohio and hitchhiked east. I saw one of Izzie's flyers in a coffee shop in Jintucket where I was staying with a friend. The flyer caught my eye because the biggest print on it said THE NO-TALENT ARTIST EXPERIMENT. I thought, 'Well, that's exactly what I am: a no-talent artist.'" Mom laughed. She's young for a mom; she's only thirty-eight, and she looks about twenty-five. Gellie's mom is almost forty-five.

Mom continues. "So I took a bus across town to her apartment — have you been there, Gellie?"

"No," says Gellie. She's wearing that blue velvet shirt I got her to buy in Jintucket. Her hair extensions are gathered in a bun on top of her head.

"Well, her place is something else," Mom says, shaking her head as she chops. "It's decorated in a very Zen way, with little furniture or clutter of any kind in any of the rooms; just a single painting on each wall. There's a sitting room just for sitting, a small kitchen for cooking and eating in, and two bedrooms with just enough room for the beds and not much else. And then there's her studio, which is huge and completely packed to the brim.

"That first evening, we did finger painting. I came in a little late, and they were all going at it, all these freaky people, all different ages. The only thing they seemed to have in common was absolutely no talent whatsoever. But they were having a blast! They were using the most amazing colors, and when somebody came across a particularly bizarre combination, they'd go around the room and share it. I remember this one guy had the most remarkable shades of yellow and royal purple that looked fabulous together, and he came up to me and offered to put some of each in my painting. I thought, 'This is unusual. Artists who share their ideas rather than jealously hoard them.' I went to that class every Sunday night for three years. And then, of course, when I got together with Randi's father . . ."

"Ooh, tell that part!" I say.

"Gellie doesn't want to hear that."

"Yeah, I do. How did you and Mr. Rankin meet?" asks Gellie. She's probably the only person on earth who calls my dad Mr. Rankin.

But just then our two cats, Roy and Leo, trot toward the door. Aunt Izzie's here. The cats run to the door when it's Aunt Izzie because she always brings them bits of dried fish tied in stems of catnip.

"Sweeeeetheart!" she exclaims, setting down her shopping bags to hug me. She smells of clay and incense. She's wearing long flowy white pants with a long white tunic, bright purple and red scarves, and a multicolored glass-bead choker necklace. Her red hair is tied back with a small black scarf and makes a kind of halo around her face. She takes my face in her hands and looks at me closely. "Are you in love?" she says. "There is nothing more beautiful than a girl in love."

She says this to me about a million times a day whenever she comes over. I wonder if she'll be able to tell when I really am in love.

"Hi, Izzie," says Gellie, grinning shyly.

"Hello, *Gellie*!" she says. Mom hugs Aunt Izzie with her fingers outstretched so she won't get paella juice on Aunt Izzie's white tunic. "Madeleine, how are you surviving in this heat?" my aunt says. "And looking so beautiful!"

"Lots of iced tea." Mom laughs, offering her a glass.

"Gellie, I hear from my sources that you are singing now," Aunt Izzie says, taking the iced tea and unpacking her shopping bags at the counter. Izzie collects department store and boutique paper shopping bags and uses them as disposable tote bags. Today there are two baguettes poking out of one of them. She also pulls out a bottle of tangerine seltzer water and a paper box from the bakery on Maple Street. She always brings us dessert from there. Today it's chocolate-edged lace cookies to go with Mom's crème brûlée.

But before Gellie can answer, Dad comes in from the living room.

"Izzie," says Dad. He is beaming. Once Mom told me that Aunt Izzie was the one person in the world whose opinion Dad cares about when it comes to his music. Dad never reads what the newspapers say about him. He says, "The good reviews are never good enough, and the bad reviews can destroy you. I'm free only if I never even look at them. That way I'm playing by my rules, not theirs."

Now he is standing in the doorway, looking small next to his older sister; I think they're actually the same size, but since Aunt Izzie's so thin, she looks taller. Plus she stands up super straight. "Yoga," she once said to explain it. "When you stand on your head, gravity makes you taller."

"I put on Gershwin for you," Dad says, jerking his thumb toward the stereo speakers. "'Someone to Watch over Me.'"

"Thanks, sweetheart," says Aunt Izzie. "My favorite."

☆ ☆ ☆

The first course of dinner is pea soup the way Mom makes it: pureed peas, with Chinese pea pods floating in it and a few unpureed English peas. Also floating in it are bits of cilantro and scallions. I'm afraid we've lost the chance to hear about how Mom and Dad met. I mean, I know how they met, but for some reason, I'm dying to have Gellie hear the story. Instead, Aunt Izzie's talking now about when she was in Morocco and was stuck on a runaway camel.

"I had to just hang on with my legs and pray to the gods," she is saying. "Camels are attached to the reins via nose rings, so you can't pull too hard on the reins or you'll tear their nostrils."

"Mom, didn't you and Dad meet in Morocco?" I say as a kind of pathetic last resort.

They all look at me.

"Honey, you know how we met," says Mom, perplexed.

"Gellie hasn't heard it." I know my face is beet red.

"Oh!" says Izzie, getting it instantly, as usual. "Well, it's a good story. See, Gellie, Randi's mother was really my most talented student."

"No," demurs Mom, smiling.

"Well, of course you were, Madeleine. She shouldn't have been in The No-Talent Artist Experiment. One of the first things she made in my class was this thrown statue. It was amazing. It had three figures — one young, one middle-aged, and one elderly. They're on a hill; the infant is crawling up, the adult is at the summit, and the old man is climbing down." Aunt Izzie puts her hand on her heart and tears come into her eyes.

I should say that Aunt Izzie cries kind of easily.

"As I recall, a piece broke off and had to be reglued before the exhibition," Mom says, remembering.

"Yes," says Aunt Izzie, wiping her eyes. Addendum: Aunt Izzie cries a lot but never for very long. "The exhibition. Now here's the amazing part: I sent that piece to my friend who owned a little gallery on Wisconsin Avenue in Jintucket. It was part of a show called Myths and Legends, and Guy went to it without knowing that any of my students were involved."

"When I saw Madeleine's piece, I was transfixed," Dad says. "I thought, 'That's the freshest thing I've ever seen.' She called it *Three Stages*."

Mom smiles again.

"And then he wrote the song!" I burst out, to break the intolerable silence, though I have to say, I'm glad to see Mom and Dad looking like they actually like each other again.

"So," Dad goes on, "I actually inquired at the gallery how much this piece cost. Where'd we put that, anyway, Madeleine?"

"How should I know?" my mom answered. "You bought it. It's your statue now."

"Anyway, the gallery owner said that it was a student's work and he was doing the teacher a favor . . ."

"Not saying that the teacher was Izzie Marquez," Aunt Izzie adds.

"So I'm persistent, and I ask who the artist is. He looks under the statue and says, 'Madeleine Harrington,' and I say I want to buy it. It cost me half my rent money for the month, but it was well worth it. I took it home and put it on my coffee table and, within twenty-four hours, I'd written my first song in months and named it 'Three Stages.'"

"This is when it gets really weird," I say to Gellie.

"So I'm doing this weekly gig at a club called The Four Elements," Dad continues. "And one night as I'm doing my set, I look out in the audience and there's this gorgeous girl with curly brown hair and a Velvet Underground T-shirt — you know, the one with Andy Warhol's banana on it. And I think, 'If I were ever to get married, I'd marry *her*.' Then I do 'Three Stages' and she gets all round-eyed. It's like she's hanging on to my every word. So at the set break, I get up the nerve to go talk to her."

Suddenly, I strangely find myself thinking about kissing Martin at the party and how it felt. And how I still haven't had a chance to tell Gellie.

"We got married within a year," says Mom. "I was twenty. My parents, of course, disowned me, cut me off completely. That was the best swap I ever made." She laughs.

I've never even met the grandparents on my mom's side. And Dad's parents are dead. It gives a person a lopsided feeling. I'm glad I have Aunt Izzie, because if I didn't, I wouldn't know any of my relatives besides Mom and Dad.

Aunt Izzie is worth at least ten relatives.

"I love Izzie," says Gellie as I walk her to the door after Aunt Izzie's gone home. "Maybe we could go over to her place sometime."

"Yeah," I say, holding the door open for her and silently willing her to leave. Mom and Dad are fighting again. It started about the dishes. Now it's about something else just as stupid. I don't want Gellie to hear them. She gives me a funny look and says, "Well, bye. See you tomorrow."

"Are we practicing 'Clairman Town'?" I ask.

"Of course!" shouts Gellie from the sidewalk. "That's all I've got on my schedule. You, me, and our guitars. Maybe we could even learn one of your dad's songs."

"Or one by this new band John introduced me to," I say. "I'll bring you their CD."

"Cool," says Gellie and runs across the street to her house.

☆ ☆ ☆

I'm cleaning up. It's hard to get the sticky baked-in sugar off the ramekins from the crème brûlée. I have the water on full force so I can't hear what they're saying. I don't need to. It'll be the usual. Mom is mad that Dad is always on the road. Dad is angry that Mom doesn't give him time or space to practice or ever want to hear his new songs when he's home. I can practically recite their fight.

"I'm left alone to raise a teenage daughter. This is not what I bargained for."

"What do you want me to do?" Dad will say.

Then Mom will throw up her hands. "That's the whole point right there! Why should I have to tell you what to do? She's your daughter! You have lots of things you like to do together. Just show up once in a while and DO them."

Which is sort of unfair. I mean, Dad does do stuff with me. But he has to be out on the road or we wouldn't have enough money and he'd be sad and depressed and have to go work for Starbucks or something. That's what he always says, anyway, at the end of every fight: "What do you want me to do, go work at Starbucks?"

"Oh, for godssakes!" Mom will make that frowny face and shut the door to their bedroom. Then Dad will go into his studio and shut the door and play Violent Femmes songs on his guitar.

Later, when I go down the hall toward my bedroom, they're back at it.

"You haven't even asked to hear what I've written on the road since I left. You haven't wanted to hear a new song of mine in five years."

"That's because I don't need to! You play them for me all the time! The one thing I can count on, in fact, the one thing I can *depend* on from you is that I'll be kept abreast of your constant stream of creativity. And you don't even know what happened to my statue!"

I shut the door to my bedroom and turn on my boom box. Bob Dylan's *Blood on the Tracks* drowns out all the noises, especially the ones coming from inside my head.

CHAPTER EIGHT

i Never Get the Frizzies!

I'm backstage at a huge theater, the kind Dad plays when he's out with Gayle Al Fresca. Gellie and I are dressed in black fishnet stockings, and both of us have red sparkles in our hair. We're about to go onstage and keep jumping up and down, all excited, and when we jump, we sort of stay up as though we're floating. Then she turns to me and says, "I want to start with 'Haven't I Been Good.'"

"I don't know that song," I say.

"Sure you do. It's only got a couple of weird chords. I'll cover for you."

And we go out onstage, but I really don't know what I'm doing, and I can't get my guitar to stay strapped on.

Essie and Shawna are in the audience and come up onto the stage and say, "Those sparkles look rococo. Don't they?" And then I notice the audience is dressed in eighteenth-century clothes and wearing white powdered wigs. They all start talking to each other, and we can't get their attention.

"Gellie's on the phone," says Mom, coming from backstage.

Then I wake up and Mom is standing by my bed with the extension phone in her hand.

"Hello," I say sleepily.

"Don't kill me," says Gellie.

It turns out Gellie can't spend the day with me and the guitars. She forgot that she and her mother are driving to Boston to audition for Silkifina's line of teen hair products. And now she's even trying to get me to come with her.

"You can bring your guitar, and we'll practice together. We'll have lots of time. You'll see. You sit around at these auditions and wait and do crossword puzzles and read magazines most of the time. Then for five minutes they call you, and you're in front of the camera. We can sneak away, and we'll probably get more practicing done than we would if we were home." Gellie is in high spirits, as though she's figured out a truly brilliant solution to her problem.

I am dubious, but since John doesn't need me today, I go along.

We're squashed together in the Volvo. Mrs. Riddle is

driving us, with Hairy Scary Margie, Jeremy the Not Boyfriend, and Flawless Barbara. Margie and Jeremy are going to watch some boring black-and-white film by an Italian director at Film Noir in Boston. Barbara's shopping for a new bathing suit.

"This is a *national* commercial," remarks Mrs. Riddle, eyeing Gellie in the rearview mirror. "If we get this, there will be residuals for years."

Gellie smiles and wiggles around like a happy puppy dog.

"What are residuals?" I ask, though I suspect they're something like Dad's royalty checks.

"That means," says Mrs. Riddle, "that every single time the commercial airs, Gellie gets *paid*, Randi. One commercial can subsidize her entire college education if she invests her residual checks as they come in."

"No matter what, I'll get free Silkifina. They give everyone who tries out a case of it," says Gellie. "Wahoo, free stuff!" and her eyes are shiny. She really does love this.

"Though we aren't really doing this for the money *or* the product," notes Mrs. Riddle. "This is just the kind of exposure I've been looking for, for Gellie. This is big. This is really big."

Mrs. Riddle's knuckles are white as they grip the steering wheel. She is bent slightly forward as we hurtle along the Mass Pike. The air-conditioning is blasting, but I'm sweltering anyway, squished in the backseat. I want to roll the window down, but I don't know if I'm allowed to.

"What are you going to do if Gellie loses?" Margie yawns. "Slit your wrists?"

"Margie!" growls Mrs. Riddle. "Gellie's not going to lose! Don't even put that thought into her head. This is a challenge. We are up for it!"

Jeremy pinches his lips together to keep from laughing, but Margie hoots out loud.

"Mom, your challenges are so pathetic! People in the Third World are starving to death. People in this country are undernourished and out of work. And you're worried about whether or not Gellie gets a stupid commercial for a hair product."

"That's enough!" snaps Mrs. Riddle. "It may not be the most important thing in the world, but it's your sister's career we're talking about here! And while you've had your easy, carefree life, your sister's been working ever since she was a baby to get to this point! And it *is* challenging, and life is about meeting challenges."

"Well, the challenge Gellie needs to meet today is how she's going to do a convincing hair commercial when her hair looks like she just stuck her finger in an electrical socket," comments Barbara nonchalantly.

"Never mind about that," says Mrs. Riddle. "I brought the blow-dryer and plenty of mousse. No one comes to a commercial audition looking perfect. We'll fix it."

But Margie is not ready to let go of her rant. "I am totally offended by your use of the word 'challenging,'" she says, turning in her seat to glare at Barbara. "I find it challenging to be in a family where the emphasis is on such shallowness. I must have been adopted."

"You were," Barbara deadpans. "I find it challenging to have to hear you turn every little annoyance into a global crisis."

Gellie seems to tune out her sisters' arguing. She is happy, and her happiness temporarily rubs off on me. For the rest of the ride, we find everything "challenging." The weather. The CD Margie insists on listening to. The smell of gas at the gas station where we fill up. We are so amused that we make up a song, which we sing at the top of our lungs. It's a sort of call and response. Gellie calls and I respond:

My baby wants a diamond ring,
I find this so challenging.
My baby thinks that she can sing,
I find this so challenging.
My baby makes peculiar sounds,
I find this so challenging.
My baby weighs two hundred pounds,
I find this so challenging.

Margie keeps yelling at us to shut up. She tells us we are offensive. Barbara does, too, but sometimes she smiles, and once she gives us a good line: "My baby's breath is like a steak / My baby ate all the birthday cake." Jeremy comments, "I think they're on the brink of writing a huge hit."

☆ ☆ ☆

The audition for the Silkifina commercial is in a studio on the tenth floor of a big building shaped like a cheese grater in downtown Boston. Barbara, Margie, and Jeremy have gone off on their own, and I am lugging my guitar about five paces behind Mrs. Riddle and Gellie, who are hurrying to make the cattle call, as Mrs. Riddle calls it, on time. Every mother and daughter in New England must be trying out for this commercial. The line all the girls are practicing is "I never get the frizzies anymore!"

There's only one problem. Because of the hair extensions — which Mrs. Riddle removed last night, figuring that if you're going to audition for a hair commercial, you should probably not have fake hair — Gellie's hair is damaged. You might even call it frizzy. Even after Mrs. Riddle dunks Gellie's head under the ladies' room sink and slathers it with mousse and blows it dry, Gellie's usually fine straight hair will not cooperate. When she says, "I never get the frizzies anymore," I have to keep my hands over my eyes and my head down to keep from cracking up.

"I'm going to find this supposed miracle product," grumbles Mrs. Riddle, leaving us alone in the ladies' room.

When she's out the door, I say, "OK. Let's practice." And I pull out my guitar. Gellie turns from the mirror and sits on the counter between two sinks. I tune up my guitar, and we sing the first lines of "Clairman Town." The sound bounces off the bathroom walls, and we sound better than I've ever heard us.

But before we can sing anymore, Mrs. Riddle is back with a bottle of Silkifina.

"What are you doing?" She yells at me. "Put that guitar away! Gellie needs to FOCUS!"

And she whirls around on Gellie and starts working on her. She plucks Gellie's eyebrows and makes her eyes stand out. Apparently, this is important. She covers Gellie's peaches and cream skin with a bronze-colored foundation and paints lipstick on her lips, making them look fuller than normal. She squirts the hair product all over Gellie's hair and runs the blow-dryer so loud and hot that I can feel it from the bathroom stall where I've retired with my guitar.

"There," says Mrs. Riddle. "That'll do for now."

I come out of the stall. I look at my face in the mirror behind Gellie's. Somehow, seeing my reflection next to hers, I look all wrong. Her almond-shaped eyes make mine look ridiculously round. My face looks swollen and puffy and blotchy next to her clear golden skin. And I have a constellation on my forehead so realistic it looks like an astrology chart. I grip the flab on either side of my waist and turn from the lightbulb-outlined mirror.

Gellie does not look like herself at all. Her face seems plastic, and she looks much older. Her nose seems too small and her eyes seem too big. She's wearing pink lipstick, black mascara, blush, eye shadow. But it's not just that she looks overly made-up; it's that she looks like she could be anyone on TV. She looks bland. Perfect but bland. Like a TV anchorwoman.

Another mother comes into the bathroom with a blonde girl, taller and thinner than Gellie, with even more makeup on.

"Don't I know you from somewhere?" the mother says to Gellie.

Mrs. Riddle smiles a huge fake smile. "Well, I don't know," she answers for her daughter.

"Hmm," says the mother, looking back and forth between Mrs. Riddle and Gellie. Mrs. Riddle has a smug look on her face. "Perhaps you've seen Angela in other commercials," Mrs. Riddle says casually. "She's done a number of ads for Fiskel and one for Barleymalt Cereal . . ."

But the woman shakes her head.

"No, I remember now. We met you all at the Miss Preteen Showboat, out in the New Haven harbor? Remember? My Becky won. I can't remember if your daughter placed or not," and the woman gives a little trill of a laugh.

Mrs. Riddle's mouth is still smiling, but her eyes and eyebrows are not cooperating.

"Yes, well. We're late for our slot," and she whisks Gellie out of the bathroom. I follow, still carrying my guitar, pretty sure Gellie's idea that we'd have tons of time to sit around and practice isn't going to happen.

This is confirmed when a tall woman with long dark hair comes barreling out of the door in the hall, with a clipboard. She looks like she's about twenty. She has a little dog, a black pug, trotting at her heels.

"Angela Riddle is next," she calls. As she goes back in the door, I hear her yell, "Where is Dede? I need her to walk Buddha if she's not going to do her job. Why am I the one doing everybody's *job*?"

And I am left behind while Gellie gets pulled into the audition room by Mrs. Riddle. Gellie's hair, unfortunately, has gone frizzy again.

I sit with the other mothers and daughters.

"Hi," I say to the girl sitting next to me. She's younger than Gellie and me, maybe in fifth grade.

She looks up at me. "I never get the frizzies anymore," she says.

"That's nice," I say.

"I never get the frizzies anymore," she repeats.

"I heard you," I say. But she turns to the person on her left and continues to repeat her line.

Across from me are another mother and daughter who look so much alike, they could practically be twins. They both have hair that looks like it's supposed to be dark brown but is the color of uncooked corn. Their eyebrows are dyed blond, too. The mother has no lines at all on her forehead. The skin around her neck is sort of wrinkly, but her face is tight, like a mask. She turns to her daughter and speaks with absolutely no emotion.

"Jennifer, if you don't get this one, you're grounded for three months. And don't think for a second you're ever going to see that boy again. You look like you haven't slept in weeks, and you've gained at least five pounds since the beginning of the month."

"Relax, Mom," says Jennifer, equally unemotional. "I'm doing the juice-fast thing. I'll have it off by the end of the week. And I don't want this commercial. I want to be a serious actress." She talks to her mother the way Barbara talks to Mrs. Riddle, as if she doesn't care what her mother thinks because she knows she's even more perfect than her mother is.

"Serious actresses know they need to pay their bills," replies the mother. "Every serious actress you've ever heard of started off in commercials."

The door opens and another young woman comes out. She has the pug on a leash and heads toward the elevator. She's probably the dark-haired woman's assistant, Dede. I take the opportunity to slip into the studio while the door is swinging shut.

Gellie is in a well-lit corner of the room, with cameras on her. Mrs. Riddle has her back to me. I'm sure Gellie can't see me because the lights are too bright.

"OK, just face the camera, and . . . GO!" says the dark-haired, now-dogless twenty-year-old.

Gellie stares into the camera and beams. "I NEVER get the frizzies anymore," and she shakes her head and runs her fingers through her uncooperative hair.

"Conrad, spray her," the dark-haired girl calls over her shoulder, and a thin guy with a goatee runs over and sprays Gellie's hair with something in a bottle that is very possibly not the miraculous Silkifina. Then he runs a brush through her hair and blows it dry. It stays straight for about five seconds and then turns to fine wires around her face. She looks kind of funky, if you ask me.

"I need a cigarette," mutters the diva in charge. "Let's get the next one in here."

"But her hair isn't always like this," Mrs. Riddle jumps up and pushes away folding chairs to get to the front of the room. "Can't you wig her? Can't you just use your *imagination*? I can show you pictures of her where her hair is perfectly straight."

"I don't have time for this. And, anyway, she's just not right. Her look's outdated. There are dozens of girls I have to see today. Do you really think I have time for a kid who doesn't even have the right hair?"

"Do you have any idea how much *experience* this child has?" cries Mrs. Riddle. "She is an absolute pro! She can do whatever is necessary, and she can and will look however you want her to look."

Gellie's face is frozen. She's looking down at her feet.

"Excuse me," says the twenty-year-old. *"Out!"* And she points to the door.

Her assistant comes back with the pug, and I slip out again. I don't want Gellie to know I saw all this. I just want to hug her. I go back to the ladies' room and play my guitar in the handicapped persons' stall.

Ten minutes later, I hear Mrs. Riddle bang the door open, and I see her feet in their pumps and Gellie's in her sneakers. I climb onto the toilet with my guitar so they can't see my feet.

"I don't want you playing music with Randi. Do you hear me?" Mrs. Riddle hisses. "You can't afford to blow another audition! You need to focus, and you need to be well rested."

"Mom, I didn't get this gig because my hair freaked out, not because I wasn't rested!" Gellie reminds her. She sounds scared.

"Well, who knows why you really didn't get this job? Those who succeed in this business do nothing but model and audition and practice. You have to be in top shape at all times and that includes total concentration. And you need friends who are going to support you in your work."

"Randi supports me," says Gellie, not very convincingly.

"Randi wants you to waste your time playing that ridiculous music," yells Mrs. Riddle. "That's fine for a completely talentless kid, but for you, Angela Riddle, it's not fine. You have much bigger fish to fry."

And they leave the bathroom. My stomach sinks. Why didn't Gellie argue with her mother? Why didn't she stick up for herself? And for me? I wait for what seems like forever to follow them out.

"Hey, excuse me, you, hey," I hear a voice behind me. It's the assistant to the pug woman.

"Yeah?" I say, turning around.

"Are you with" — and she looks down at the pad of paper she has on top of the box she's carrying — "Angela Riddle?"

"Yes," I say. Maybe they're going to call her back for one more tryout.

"Well, here's her box of product. Sorry she didn't get the job. Tell her to keep trying," says the girl.

"I will," I say. And I carry the box to the Riddles' Volvo.

"Well, this was a learning experience, wasn't it, girls? Everyone has a bad-hair day!" Mrs. Riddle laughs as if she just said the funniest thing ever. No one else laughs. Barbara, Margie, and Jeremy have no idea what happened except that Gellie didn't get the job. As for Gellie, I expect her to say something to me, but instead she won't make eye contact. She is silent for the rest of the drive home. It's almost dark when the Volvo pulls into the driveway.

"See you," says Gellie. But she doesn't even look at me.

CHAPTER NINE

Fob Richard

Most days, John brings his Powerbook out to the table in front of the store to work on his screenplay, something about British football and a character named Fob Richard. He chats with the locals who sit at the table and chairs drinking coffee, spillovers from Java Bomb, the coffee shop two doors down, because it's a good business tactic to make as many friends in Jintucket as possible.

"So when Wal-Mart comes in, I'll have some loyalty from the punters at the caff," he says. He's obsessed with the possibility that Wal-Mart or something like it will swallow his business and he'll go under and have to go back to England and live with his mother.

But today it's raining and no one is outside, including John, which I'm glad about, because when he's outside, he expects me to be inside and then I don't get to talk to him.

"What's up with your dad, Randi?" says John. "When's he coming out with a new record, hmm?"

John looks as cute as ever, wearing a navy-blue Yosemite Sam T-shirt. I love the way it hangs over his jeans. I was waiting for him to talk to me, hoping he would. But I don't want to talk about this! Dad's written twenty-three unrecorded songs. He says it's like having children who are cooped up in a dungeon.

"I don't know. But I listened to that CD you gave me," I say as I put the new releases onto racks in the front of the store. "I like that band."

"The Big Idea?" says John. He's sitting behind the cash register, reading a copy of *Rolling Stone,* then looks up and crosses his red high-top sneakers on top of the counter. "I knew you'd like them. They're brilliant. I'm sure you've seen them around. Everyone in Jintucket knows them. Most of them are members of the Becket family. They're local heroes. Rhodie's a mate of mine."

Rhodie. The dark-haired one with the braids. She plays guitar, according to the liner notes.

The door jingles but I don't turn around.

"Well, if it isn't Miss Jellybean," says John, not getting up from his stool.

"Hello," says Gellie.

"How'd you get here?" I ask, pretending to be engrossed in my sorting project.

"Rode my bike," says Gellie. "Hey, I'm sorry about the other day, not being able to rehearse and all."

I just grunt.

"I really thought we'd be able to."

"Well, we couldn't, could we?" I say, trying to pretend I don't care so much. "You obviously had much more important things going on."

"Randi, I'm sorry! You were there! You saw how crazy it was!"

Now I whirl around. "Yeah, well, I *did* see how crazy it was, so I don't even know why you even do it. What's the point? Why do you let your mom drag you into all that, anyway?"

"Shock! Horror!" says John. And he slips off his stool and goes to the back of the store.

"Lay off!" Gellie says. "I did the best I could! I'm not going to give up my whole life's worth of work just to play guitar and sing with you, OK? I can do both! Quit yelling at me!"

I turn back to my box of CDs, fuming. I hate her right now. She can just take her pretty face and amazing voice and go be the next Miss America. "You can't do both. Not really. They are complete opposites of each other. One thing is your mother's and the other is yours."

"No, one thing is my mother's and mine, and one thing is *yours* and mine. They're both *mine*."

Gellie and I glare at each other. I go back to sorting through my box of CDs. Gellie browses through the bins.

Then John starts singing in the back room, and he's getting louder and louder. He's making up words to a crazy song about Fob Richard and how Fob Richard's mom makes Fob Richard be in beauty pageants. My eyes meet Gellie's, and though we both try to keep a straight face, we start giggling. I struggle to unsmile.

"Hey, this is the CD you lent me," says Gellie, picking up the Big Idea album on John's counter, trying to make peace with me. "I listened to it yesterday. I couldn't get it out of my CD player. It's really good."

"Hmm," I say.

"Will you put it on?" she says, taking it out of its jewel case.

I don't answer at first. I'm trying to stay mad but suddenly have a hard time remembering what I'm angry about. I know deep down that Gellie really did want to rehearse with me that day.

I get up, put the CD in the shop's stereo, and press PLAY. It's a song called "Paris." Gellie starts singing along. She sings softly at first, then louder. Her voice is clear, and rings through the brick walls of Real Tunes. She's already learned all the words. When the chorus comes in, I join her, singing a harmony along with the other girl singer in the band.

The song ends on an acoustic guitar solo. It's delicate and pretty, and I start to wonder how it is played.

"You girls filled this shabby little pop joint with music from the spheres," says John. He is leaning on the door frame in the back, his arms crossed.

I blush. "Would you teach me how to play that song?" I say.

"Of course. And if I can't figure out the chords, I'll ring Rhodie up, and we'll get it straight from the source."

"Wow!" says Gellie. "You know the actual person who wrote that song?"

John laughs. "Yeah, I know the incredibly famous Rhodie Becket."

I scowl at Gellie. "You never acted that amazed about knowing my dad," I mutter, my bad mood creeping back.

"How do you know?" Gellie snaps. "Why would I fawn all over your dad in front of you? That would be weird. For all you know, I have a poster of him behind my closet door and I say good night to him before I go to sleep!"

"Ew!" I say. But Gellie is laughing, and so am I.

"You know, ladies, you should record yourselves singing. Don't you know someone who can tape you? Because if you had a recording, I could pass it around and you could maybe get some gigs."

Gellie and I look at each other.

"You really think we're good?" I say.

"From just us singing along to a CD?" Gellie says doubtfully.

John shrugs. "Dunno. I'm just saying, make a recording. I'll ring some people up for you, you know what I mean?"

"Duge does this kind of thing," I mention. "He has a little recording system. He taped the school singing group last year. He would totally help us out. Of course, he would lay down and *die* for you, Gellie."

This is the test. If Gellie will work with Duge, then I know she's really into the idea of the band. She looks away, out the window to the rainy day. A woman goes by with a yellow umbrella hat on her head. Gellie turns back.

"Call him up," she says. "Let's get started."

"Yippee!" I shout, totally acting ten years old. Then I settle down and turn to John. "So?"

"So?" John says, coming over to check my sorting job to make sure I'm not what he calls a slider.

"So? Say we get you a great recording of us. Then what?"

"So . . . ooo . . . ooo. Hmm. Well. You two are underage, I'm assuming."

I nod doubtfully.

"So that rules out heaps of places. The Catty Corner's out. Too bad the old Four Elements Café closed down. That would've been perfect for you, plus I know the bloke who used to run it. . . . Oh, wait, I know. You could do a show at that place in West Jintucket, the May Day Café,

I think it's called. They don't pay brilliantly, but they pass the hat, and people make good tips there. It's tight getting in, though, so I can't promise anything. But the owner had a little thing for me, and she may bump up your tape for a listen if I give her a call."

I don't know whether to be excited at the prospect of getting a gig or bummed out by the fact that John might have dated the owner of the May Day Café. I bet she's tall and thin with long curly red hair. I bet she reads Nietzsche. I bet she has her tongue pierced. I decide it doesn't matter as long as she lets us play.

CHAPTER TEN

Independence Day

D ad is back for two days; then he's going to be gone again. We pick him up at the airport and then go out to our favorite restaurant, the Greek Taverna in Clairman. Mom has a glass of wine and Dad and I drink Cokes. Dad hasn't had a drink in years. He says he used to drink way too much.

We're having a great time. Dad is starting to talk about songwriting.

Our food arrives at that moment: Mom and Dad both have little Crock-Pots with lamb. I'm eating chicken shish kebab. I give Mom the feta cheese and Dad the olives from the salad that came with dinner.

"First there's the creative part," Dad continues, "the part that's out of your control. It's your higher power giving you that juice. You can't squeeze it yourself. But then there's the part you can control, you can get better at with hard work. You can do your sit-ups."

"Like how you try to write a song every day?" I ask, pulling the chicken and zucchini off the stick.

"Exactly," says Dad. "First thing in the morning, I write a song. Doesn't matter if it's good or bad, it's what I do without fail. I take thirty minutes. At the end of thirty minutes, I put down the guitar and have breakfast, no matter what the song looks like."

"Except on the mornings when you don't," counters Mom.

"What are you talking about?" says Dad. I keep cutting my chicken, even though it's already in small pieces.

"I'm talking about the days when you don't adhere to your little discipline and instead sleep late because you were out all night with Gayle Al Fresca and her band," says Mom.

"Well, yeah, when I've been playing the night before," says Dad. "You can't expect me to get home at two in the morning and then get up at seven. But on those days, I do try to fit it in whenever I can. You know that."

"Yes," Mom agrees, and for a moment there is a silence when we all just chew. But then Mom continues. "You go off on your tours and leave the pesky little tasks of, oh, cooking and cleaning and making sure your daughter is clothed and educated and loved to us mere mortals. Not to mention not bothering to pick up the phone to call your wife."

This is not exactly a new conversation. But usually it takes a week after Dad gets home for them to have it. When he first comes back, they tend to be all lovey-dovey. I guess because Dad is going to go away in two days, everything is on fast-forward.

"Madeleine." Dad puts down his fork and knife. "Could we just have a nice meal here? On my one night home, can't I enjoy a little peaceful family time?"

Oh, no.

Mom shoves her crock of lamb halfway across the table and hisses, "You abandon us for weeks on end, and then you expect us to welcome you back with open arms and huge smiles on our faces? Let's see how you feel when I walk out on you." And she storms out of the restaurant without her purse.

I look at my baby-bite-sized chicken sitting stupidly on its little hill of rice pilaf.

"Don't worry, sweetheart," says Dad. "She's not going far."

"I know."

"That's just the way she is, your mom. She feels things strongly and passionately and quickly, and she blows. But she comes back her usual cheerful self. That's just the way she is."

Sure enough, Mom comes back ten minutes later

after walking around the block. She kisses me on top of my head.

"I'm sorry," she whispers. She sits down next to Dad and holds his hand tightly. She and Dad look into each other's eyes for a long time.

"We need to get away. Together," she says. Dad just nods. I want to know if Mom is talking about me, too; if I'm included. But I don't ask.

Even though I'm not actually paid at work, I'm making out like a bandit. John gives me all sorts of free stuff: CDs, posters, gizmos to open CDs with. My favorite is a poster of The Big Idea, which I brought home and hung on the wall above my bed. All the band members are interesting looking, but my favorite is Rhodie. She has a fierce look, as though she'd be willing to do anything for the people in her band. But even though her eyes are intense, there's a little half smile on one side of her mouth. Like she's sharing a joke with me.

Every day after work, John gives me a guitar lesson. He says I'm making terrific progress. I've been practicing guitar like he tells me to: playing along with the Big Idea's CD and also learning some other songs. I have a loose-leaf notebook full of them. At the end of every lesson, he gives me a guitar pick. I have fourteen now. All different colors and styles. My favorite is the black one with the little ridges.

I'm home practicing, trying to figure out a song. I get

one of the chords wrong. I'm so frustrated that I just start banging on my guitar, but then some words pop into my head, and I play the chord the right way and sing:

When I let you into my closet.

And I realize I'm writing a song. It begins with just one line and a little guitar riff to go with it. While I'm writing, this fast current carries me along. It's the best feeling I've ever had.

☆ ☆ ☆

Mom and I are invited to the Riddles' for dinner. It's the Fourth of July, and Dad's gone again. It's hot in a good way, the kind that gives you energy, as opposed to when the heat is wet and pulls you down and leaves you worn-out like a wet rag.

Mom and I go across the street together, carrying an apple pie and some hot-dog buns. Dr. Riddle, Gellie's mostly silent father, is sitting under the maple tree in a lawn chair in the backyard, reading a biography about President Harry Truman that's the size of the phone book. Mrs. Riddle is standing in front of the grill. The coals are still black. Mrs. Riddle offers Mom a glass of lemonade, and they start talking about Clairman Country Day. They get into a discussion about which play should be put on next fall, and they've practically cast it when Gellie and I sneak away to practice in her studio.

"I have a line for a song," I blurt out as soon as the door is closed behind us. "'When I let you into my closet.'"

"I've seen your closet," she says.

"No, that's the line."

"'When I let you into my closet'?" she repeats.

"Yup. Listen to what I've got so far. I know it's really dumb and all, but it's my first song."

When I let you into my closet
Right behind the leopard-skin coat

"But I can't think of anything good to rhyme with 'coat.' Boat. Note. Wrote. Float. Goat. Moat. Tote . . ."

"Remote!" says Gellie. "Hey! Let me see." And she grabs a pad and her gel pens. She scribbles furiously.

Will you still revere and adore me?
Will you just become more remote?
Will you see the actual me
And will you walk away?
Will you see what I've been hiding and tell me it's OK?

"Cool!" I say, amazed. "But what chords should we use for the 'will you see the actual me' part?"

"Hmm," says Gellie, and she fools around on her guitar. She plays a bunch of chords that don't make any sense to me. Then she adds the words, and even though it's weird, it works. In fact, it's way cooler than anything I would have made up. Gellie knows less about music than I do, but sometimes I think that makes her more creative than I am. I know the rules, and I follow them. Gellie doesn't know the rules, so she makes up her own.

"Also," she says excitedly, "I have a chorus that I was working on last week that might be good here." And she plays and sings.

Show me a sign, give me a key,
Tell me that you love me for me.
I want to be who I really am,
Maybe that'll fit into your plans,
Maybe that'll fit into your plans.

"That's great!" I shout.

"It is, isn't it?" She is bouncing up and down from her seat on the floor.

"We wrote a song! Together!" I yell, reaching up to slap her hand.

And we sing it again and again, getting more and more excited and giddy with each repetition. We write a second verse, about a locker combination. We're beginning to sound like we fit together. Also, our guitar playing is beginning to match almost as well as our voices.

"Let's sing it for them!" I say. Gellie looks up at me midway through a strum and nods. We scramble upstairs and outside to the backyard. Mom is putting charred hot dogs on a platter. Dr. Riddle is still reading his Truman book, and Mrs. Riddle is drinking out of a tall martini glass and telling Mom something about her Broadway days.

"Mom," I say, panting a little from the stairs. "Wait'll you hear our song!"

Mom's eyes light up, and she puts the platter down on the table.

"Well, go ahead and sing it for us, then. Is that OK, June?"

Mrs. Riddle puts her drink down slowly. She says, "Fine. It's time for Margie and Barbara to appear and pretend to be a part of this family, anyway." Then she goes to the screen door and in a hoarse bark calls, "Girls!"

☆ ☆ ☆

We sing the new song to Mom and the Riddles. Mom sits on the raised brick wall, Dr. Riddle in his lawn chair, Mrs. Riddle standing in the doorway to the house as if she's going to duck inside any minute. Margie is at the picnic table, filling out forms for fall internships, and Barbara is across from her with the cordless telephone in her hand. Only Mom gives us her full attention. Dr. Riddle has his Truman book closed, but I notice his finger keeps edging in between the pages, as if he's somehow reading it in Braille.

We're nervous. We've never performed together in front of anyone before, let alone our families. I stand to the left, and Gellie's on the right. Of course, there are no microphones, so we both just try to sing as loud as possible.

When I let you into my closet
Right behind the leopard-skin coat

Gellie and I are jittery for the first verse. I remember, a little too late, Mrs. Riddle's rant when Gellie didn't get the commercial. She'll probably hate this. But when we get to the chorus, I feel Gellie loosen up next to me. Her voice opens up, and she starts to belt. I close my eyes and let my body move along with my guitar. I forget about Mrs. Riddle.

I want to be who I really am,
Maybe that'll fit into your plans,
Maybe that'll fit into your plans.

We practically scream that last line. We are both bouncing around the patio by the second verse.

When I give you my combination
Will you keep it all to yourself?
Will you leave me poems and candy,
Will you tell it to somebody else?
Will you make me into a fool
Or will you hold my hand?
When I tell you that I am lonely
Will you understand?

When we're done, Margie says, "That wasn't bad. You're going to be the next Angry Young Waifs. In fact, you should call yourselves that — Angry Young Waifs.

Can we eat already? Jeremy and I are going to Jintucket to watch the fireworks."

From Margie, this is a compliment.

Barbara puts the phone next to her ear, gets up, and continues her conversation. But I think I saw a flicker of appreciation in her flawless face.

Dr. Riddle clears his throat and says, "Very good." Then he opens his book again.

Mom claps and claps, her eyes shining. "I can't believe you wrote that! That is a fine, fine song! I want you to play it for Guy when he gets home, OK? And girls! Your voices! They just soar! Your *blend*! You two are so sweet together."

Mrs. Riddle says with a sniff, "I didn't know people still listened to folk music."

"Well, it's not really folk music." Mom stiffens. "More pop folk. It's exactly the kind of music my husband makes."

"And he makes a living doing this?" Mrs. Riddle asks.

Mom's jaw drops, but Margie intervenes before Mom can say anything.

"Yeah, Mom, and that's the only reason Gellie and Randi are singing for you today," says Margie, rolling her eyes. "They see a way to become bazillionaires, and they're going for it."

Mrs. Riddle glowers. "I don't want Gellie getting distracted by *any* music," she says. "You never know when something's going to come through for her. She has a very full career, you know."

☆ ☆ ☆

During dinner, Mrs. Riddle drones on and on about Gellie's career, Barbara's chances of getting into Princeton, and Margie's unfulfilled potential at Yale. Dr. Riddle cuts up his hot dogs with a knife and fork and ignores the buns we brought. Mom and Margie talk about acupuncture, which is the high point of the discussion, but it ends when Dr. Riddle asks if acupuncture is like chiropractic. Gellie doesn't say anything and won't look at me. She looks defeated, like a wet dog. We performed together for the first time, we just wrote our very first song together, and I feel like her mother's pushed her further away from Plastic Angel. We should be celebrating our independence today.

The moment she finishes her last bite of pie à la mode, my mother jumps up from the table.

"Well, Randi, we'd better get back so we're home when your father calls after sound check. Thank you all so much for dinner." And we leave together, me with my guitar and Mom with the leftover apple pie. The temperature is still hot, even though the sun is well behind the trees. When we are at the end of the Riddles' driveway, I hiss, "I hate Mrs. Riddle! Someone should come and take her children away from her before it's too late for them."

Mom is quiet for a long minute. "She's had kind of a hard time, Randi. Give her a break. It's not easy being a mom."

"But why does that entitle her to keep Gellie from having a life?"

We've come to the front door of our house now. The cats rub up against my leg, and I stoop down to scratch their ears. Mom hasn't answered my question. She puts the pie in the refrigerator.

"Probably," Mom says finally, "because she doesn't feel like *she* gets to have one." She picks up the phone to see if there's a voice mail message from Dad. I know there's not, because she hangs up and her lips form a straight line.

"He's probably going to call when the set's over," she says. "But I'm too tired to wait up. Good night, sweetheart." And she kisses me on the top of the head.

I'm in bed when the phone rings, only once. Through the walls I hear Mom crying.

CHAPTER ELEVEN

The Agents

"**T**erry Duganton here," Duge answers the phone curtly.

"Hey," I say. "It's Randi."

"What's doing?"

"I'm wondering if you want to record Plastic Angel's first record," I say.

"Huh," says Duge. "I think I could manage that. Come on up to my studio. I've taken over the lighting booth at school, and all my stuff's up there."

Duge is the theater teacher's right-hand man. He has the keys to the building and is the only one on campus who knows how to work the light and sound systems at the school.

"You're a prince," I say. "I owe you."

"The pleasure is mine. Name the day, and I'll make sure I'm there."

I called Duge to keep the momentum of Plastic Angel going. Ever since the Fourth of July party, Gellie's had to be more secretive about practicing. We lie low around Mrs. Riddle and mostly practice at my house. Today, we're listening to the Big Idea CD and scouring the liner notes for clues.

"I like the guy with the glasses best," says Gellie. "And the blonde girl singer. But Rhodie looks scary."

"That's because she's a real artist," I say. "She's the writer in the band. Plus, she plays the guitar."

I explain who's who. "Peter's the guy with the glasses, the guitar player. He's the oldest brother. Rhodie is the middle sister, and Zhsanna, the blonde singer, is the youngest. Jack's the tall guy — he plays bass."

"Do you think we'll ever get famous like that?" Gellie asks.

"I don't know. Dad says it's not all it's cracked up to be."

"It's weird to think about your parents as being actual people," Gellie says. "Like, it freaks me out to think about when my mom was in show business. That's so not her today."

"Was your mom really *that* into show business?" I say.

"Yeah, until she had me."

"Wait," I say. "I thought she gave up her Broadway thing way back when she married your father."

"She did. Then she had Margie and Barbara. Right before I came along, she was going to try to get back into show business. I was kind of an accident, I guess."

"She told you that?"

"Yeah. She's said it a few times. 'If I hadn't had you, I'd be sending out my own eight-by-tens.' Of course, then she always tells me I'm way more beautiful than she ever was and that she'd much rather have me than a career."

We strum through the chords to the song. It's not too hard, just lots of chord changes, but nothing we can't handle. I look up at the poster of The Big Idea and focus on Rhodie above my bed. She's got her eyes half closed and her mouth half open. Now she looks like she's sharing a joke with Gellie.

After we've run through the song a few times, I say, "What do you think you're going to be doing ten years from now?"

Gellie blinks. "What do I *think* I'll be doing or what do I *want* to be doing?"

"What do you *want* to be doing?"

There's a long pause. Then she takes a deep breath. "This," she whispers. "But I'm afraid to tell my mom."

This is huge. Gellie's never put singing before modeling before.

We play some more until Gellie breaks a string. We need to go to her house to get a new one.

"I talked to Duge," I mention as we're crossing the street.

"So?"

"So, he says he'll record us. He's got the key to the lighting booth at school and has a recording system all set up for us."

"Wow," says Gellie. "We're going to have a CD."

"And then we'll be massively famous. The kids in school will be so freaked. I hope they don't all start to hate us just because we're amazing."

"They won't," says Gellie. "They will only fear and respect us."

"Soon we will achieve world domination. Mwah-ha-ha."

"I'm actually beginning to look forward to going back to school," Gellie admits.

"You?" I say incredulously.

"Yeah, me. I think I could make friends this year. Essie seemed pretty friendly."

"Wow," I say. "There's hope for you."

"What's that quote by Emily Dickinson you have up on your wall? 'Hope is the thing with feathers'? We have to have hope!" And she shouts into the blue sky. "I am going to make friends! And we are going to be a great rock-and-roll band! Angels! Plastic and otherwise! Are you listening?"

"Are you listening?" I repeat, leaping onto the curb on Gellie's side of the street.

We notice a silver Audi in her driveway. "Whose car?" I say.

"Beats me," says Gellie. "It's fancy schmancy."

Mrs. Riddle opens the door, flushed and excited. She must have seen us coming.

"Just in time," she squeals. "Just in time! Gellie, look who came to pay us a visit!"

A strange-looking couple are in the living room. They look like twins. The woman has slicked-back blond hair with her dark roots just showing, in a way that's stylish and on purpose, not because she hasn't had time to visit the salon. The man has dark brown hair, also slicked back, with a slightly receding hairline. Other than that, almost everything about them is identical. They have very tanned skin that shines like brass. They have deep-set eyes that look all glimmery but sort of cold. They wear black turtlenecks with silver-gray designer jeans, very tight, and pointy boots.

"Hello, little lady," says the man, coming toward Gellie with his arms outstretched.

"Hi," says Gellie, letting herself be hugged. "This is my friend Randi."

The man shakes my hand with just the tips of his fingers. Dad told me never to trust anyone who shakes hands that way.

He says to me, "Hello, Brandy." And then he turns back to Gellie. "Allow me to introduce myself and my partner in all things. We are Steve and Boo Hines. We've come here to talk about representing you, though in just a half hour, sitting with June here, it seems like we've already been working together for a long time, doesn't it, June?" This he says to Mrs. Riddle, who nods enthusiastically and agrees that it seems like they've all been chummy forever.

"THE NEW SHOTS ARE EXQUISITE," says Boo, putting the emphasis on the "ex" of "exquisite" so that it sounds like "eggs." She barks everything she says as if we're all slightly deaf. "YOU ARE JUST DRIPPING WITH TALENT, YOUNG LADY, DRIPPING WITH TALENT."

"Oh, yes, we are so excited about your new head shots," Steve says, grinning. His teeth are bizarrely white. "We've gotten some very positive feedback from our people. Very positive feedback."

The woman nods her head vigorously in agreement. "THINGS ARE GONNA START HAP-PEN-ING," she says with a singsong.

"Really," says Gellie. "Like what?"

"Well, for starters, Missy, we've got an audition for you next week in New York. For Graceline's new Jeune Femme collection. Their rep called us this morning and said you'd be perfect."

"Why does she have to go to New York, then?" I blurt out. "If they already know she'll be perfect."

Everyone stares at me. I don't care. I'm scared she's going to have to do this stupid audition and miss recording with Duge.

"BECAUSE . . . what's your name, again, dear?"

"Randi," I mutter.

"BECAUSE, BRANDY, THEY NEED TO GET A SENSE OF HOW SHE'LL WORK WITH *OTHERS*."

Boo is speaking to me like I'm either really young or mildly brain-damaged. *And* deaf.

Steve clears his throat. "What my partner means is that Gellie is being groomed so that what happened in *Boston*" — he whispers the city as though it were a bad word — "never has to happen again. We are going to teach her how to audition so that when she gets her next chance in front of a casting director, she will be guaranteed the role. What we have here, in rough form, is a brand-new baby star. This one is going *far*." And he sticks both his forefingers out at Gellie like they're little guns.

Mrs. Riddle looks at me dangerously. "Gellie's career is about to take a very exciting turn," she says, stroking Gellie's head as if her daughter were a Pomeranian. "You're going to be happy for your friend when she gets her big break, aren't you, dear?"

And I'm forced to nod. Who wouldn't with those little guns pointed at you?

CHAPTER TWELVE

The Demo

It's weird to be at school in the middle of summer. You notice all the summer noises in a new way, like the sounds of the insects buzzing or the lawn mower going. It's hot and hazy, and wavy lines in the air make the school buildings look like a mirage. The principal and dean of students and their secretaries are around, but they're dressed in shorts and T-shirts and look almost like normal people. They smile and say, "How's the summer going?" and don't seem to realize how strange and out of place they look. I'm kind of embarrassed for them.

"You do know that Duge is going to show up and sit at your feet and fawn all over you," I say. We're running through our song in front of the locked theater, waiting for Duge.

"Oh, great. I hope not," says Gellie, looking around nervously and distractedly messing with her hair.

"You have such gigantic problems," I say. "You have a boy head over heels for you. I feel totally sorry for you." I *still* haven't told her about Martin. Not that Martin's called me once since the party. Not that I care. Much.

"Shut up!" says Gellie, blushing. "It isn't *boys*, it's *Duge*. He's a bando, remember?"

"So?"

"So. All your so-called popular friends think he's the biggest dork ever."

"So what? It doesn't matter what they think. It only matters what *you* think," I scold her. But then I think about Essie's face when she talked about Duge's sweaty palms. Would I be able to stop caring what they thought?

Maybe I would. If the person I liked were really worthy.

"Don't you like him at all?" I say.

"Of course, I like him," says Gellie. "He's essentially likable and all. But . . . ," her voice trails off.

"Maybe you just don't want him to see what's in your closet," I say wickedly. "So you keep him at arm's length." And I play the song on my guitar to prove my point.

We're getting into the song, singing louder and louder. Images of us onstage at our first gig flit through my head, of all the kids looking up at us, amazed and intimidated, dancing. No, not dancing, just kind of mesmerized. Gellie is grinning at me as we sing together. She and I play the riff at the same time and then she plays a harmony riff on her guitar while I play the melody on mine.

"Cool!" I shout.

"I've been practicing." She smiles.

Duge appears on his bicycle, riding over the hill that leads up to the theater building. He parks it and comes over, carrying a backpack full of cables and microphones. Then he takes his bike helmet off, which makes his hair stand up even worse than usual.

"Ladies," he says, bowing slightly and tripping over his big brown shoes. He flushes when he looks up at Gellie. "Let's get started."

"Check, check," says Duge into each mike. There are four altogether: one each for our voices, one each for our guitars. Duge has a mixing console at the back of the lighting booth, which is in a loft that hangs above the theater. He sets up a little corner for each of us, trying to baffle the different sounds with some foamlike stuff that looks like gigantic egg cartons. I'm in my own little fort with my two mikes. Gellie is in hers.

Duge is an amazing musician. Besides being able to play *any* instrument, he knows all about the electronic stuff that musicians need, which he calls gear. Stuff like amps and cables and processors and recording devices. I'm glad we have Duge. He can be in Plastic Angel, too, as far as I'm concerned.

Duge checks the mike in front of Gellie. "That guitar is gigantic," he says. "You should be playing a smaller one."

"Thanks a lot," says Gellie. "I know that. But where am I going to get the money to get my dream guitar?"

"Don't you get money from your modeling gigs?" asks Duge.

"Well, yeah," says Gellie. "But can you imagine how my mom would react if I spent my modeling money on a new guitar?"

While we wait for Duge to run the cables back and forth between us and his console, I come out of my fort to visit Gellie in hers. Gellie is supposed to be taking her measurements for an application Boo and Steve sent her, so she has a tape measure and is awkwardly stretching it around her body parts. I help her. After we do her hips, bust, and waist, we decide to measure every single measurable body part on both of us, just for the heck of it.

"Two and a half inches," says Gellie holding the tape measure up to my ear. "How long are mine?"

I hold the tape measure up to Gellie's right ear. "Two and three-quarters," I say.

"Weird," says Gellie. "I am so much shorter than you, but all of my facial features are bigger."

Next we measure the length of our faces, from hairline to chin. Mine is seven inches. Gellie's is seven and a half.

"Do you want reverb?" Duge calls to us from behind the mixing console.

We both jump, totally startled, and Gellie rushes to stash the tape measure.

"What's that?" says Gellie as I scamper back to my corner.

"Umm," says Duge. "Basically, it makes you sound richer and lush, kind of like how you sound when you sing in the shower."

"Yeah!" says Gellie. "That's how I sound best!"

"OK," says Duge. "Sing something. Anything. I need to check levels."

So we sing through "Clairman Town," which Duge says is his favorite song ever. Then we sing a Big Idea song called "When I'm Here."

"That sounds amazing!" yells Duge, clapping his hands together from behind the console. "You guys are so righteous!" It sounds kind of weird for Duge to use a word like "righteous." But I'll take it.

"Did you write that song?" he asks, coming out from behind the console and sitting on the floor with his back against the wall.

"Nope. Big Idea song," I say. As usual, I know about a cool, obscure band before everyone else does.

"I want to see them sometime," says Duge.

"You should," says Gellie. "They're great."

"I guess you don't need to go out for any more commercials now, huh, Gellie," says Duge.

"What do you mean?" asks Gellie, stiffening and avoiding my eyes.

"I mean," says Duge, "now you have a way of being famous that's way cooler than being a teen model. Now you can be a rock star."

"I'm not being a model to get famous," Gellie snaps, her eyes on fire.

"Well, then, what are you being a model for?"

"Because," says Gellie. She doesn't answer for a while. I think of all the reasons Gellie might want to be a model. Her mom makes her and she's too scared to quit. She's good at it. Or, she's lying and she really does want to get famous as a model. Maybe she wouldn't know she was beautiful without all those people telling her all the time. I don't really know. I just know that it's a really tender area, like a bruise, and that Duge is poking at it. Still, I need to hear what she has to say, the way you sometimes have to listen when your parents are fighting.

"It's sort of like, what I *do*. I mean, my sister Margie's the brain, and my sister Barbara's the jock. I'm the model. It's my thing," she says finally. "And I like it. It's fun. I might even go to Hollywood."

"You're going to Hollywood?" Duge is surprised.

So am I. Not in a good way.

Gellie continues not to look at me. "Maybe. I have these new agents, Boo and Steve. They say there's a good chance that I'm going to get to go to California to try out for this movie, and that I'm perfect for this one role."

"Cool! You're going to be a movie star!" says Duge.

"She can have two careers," I say, suddenly gaily and a

little too loudly to prove this news doesn't bother me. "Just like J.Lo." I check my watch. "Come on, you guys. I have to get back to Real Tunes before John kills me. Let's do another song."

"Do that pretty one," suggests Duge.

"Big Idea's 'Haven't I Been Good'?" I say.

"Yeah, that."

I shake my head. "I don't know it," I say.

"It's easy," says Gellie.

Not for me. I think it's really hard, and I barely know how to play the chords. But I've always wanted to try the two-part harmony Rhodie and Zhsanna Becket do. But Gellie sings and plays it by herself.

As Gellie sings through it, I feel embarrassed that she knows it so much better than I do. But I sing along on the chorus and by the last verse I get most of the harmony. I try to concentrate on the sound of our two voices together and that magical way we can get them to ring.

But now the thought that Gellie might go to Hollywood is hovering over my head. I want her to stay here and sing with me so badly there's a lump in my throat. I don't want to share her with Mrs. Riddle. I don't want her to have two careers.

We record every single song we know. Duge promises to mix them for us and give us each a CD by the end of the week.

"Wouldn't it be cool if we could really make an album?" I say when we're finished singing the last song.

"What do you think we're doing here?" says Duge, wrapping up the cables.

But I think back to the days when Dad would take me with him to the fancy studio in New York, back when he was on a big-deal record label. I would sit in the seats that twirled around and look out the window on the fifteenth floor and play with the cats that lived in the studio. The studio walls were lined with tightly wound carpeting, and one of the cats could actually climb the walls. Dad called it Velcro Cat.

"No, I mean a real record," I say. "With background instruments, drums, fancy artwork on the cover."

Gellie picks up her modeling application and shakes the papers together and puts them in her bag. "We'll do that someday," she says. "And someday I'll have my dream guitar. It's good to dream."

CHAPTER THIRTEEN

Bollocks

We don't practice again for days after the recording. Mrs. Riddle, Boo, and Steve have Gellie in a whirlwind of activity at all times.

"I can't today," says Gellie when I ask. "I spent all day yesterday at a seminar with Boo and Steve on how to maximize my head shots, and I'm exhausted. I should stay home and rest." We're standing by my mailbox. As usual, there's no mail for me, just bills for my mom and music catalogues for my dad.

"Then how about tomorrow?" I'm trying to be calm. Gellie never having time to practice makes the back of my neck hurt.

"Tomorrow I have to fly to New York for auditions for the Graceline commercial," says Gellie.

"Well, just let me know when you're free," I say, trying to turn elegantly to head inside. Instead, I trip over the hem of my bell-bottom and drop all the mail.

"Randi."

"What," I mutter, gathering up the envelopes.

"Maybe over the weekend I could meet you at Real Tunes. Duge should have the CDs by then, and we can give one to John."

"Fine," I say, not quite willing to let go of my sulk. But I feel a tiny bit better.

I go in the house, toss the mail on the kitchen counter, and head straight upstairs for my bedroom. I pull out my guitar and play the beginning of a new song Gellie wrote before Boo and Steve took over her life. We hadn't learned it in time for the recording. Maybe we'll never sing it together. But I can sing it by myself.

Longest shadow I have known
It's time to let you go.
All these trains you put me on
They move too slow
They're almost paralyzed
You didn't realize
And I should have let you know
I could fly if I wanted to.

"Where'd you hear that?" It's Dad. I didn't know he was home from his tour. Lately, he's been coming and going so often, I can't keep track.

I shrug. "Gellie." I don't want to tell him that we actually made a CD or about Plastic Angel.

But he doesn't ask about the band. Instead, he nods, distracted. "It's a nice melody," he says. He sits on the end of my bed. "Who's it about?"

"No one," I say. I hand Dad the guitar. He shakes his head. "You play," he says. So I play "Sara with Your Ring," one of his songs.

He smiles ruefully. "They passed on that one," he says when I'm done playing.

The back of my neck twinges. "Bummer," I say. "Well, what do they know?"

"That it's not going to make three million dollars," Dad says shortly. "It's too quirky. Too interesting. 'You have to dumb it down, Guy' is what I always hear."

I run my pick over the bass string, making it buzz.

"Sometimes I hate the music business," I say.

Dad looks at me and opens his mouth like he's going to tell me something. Then shuts it and shakes his head. He gets up to leave. "Don't hate the business, Randi. It's hard, but it's the best business in the world. It lets a whole lot of those of us who need to make music make music. It's not anyone's fault that people want to hear dumb songs. If you hate the music biz, that's like saying you hate people.

And that's not where you want to be. You don't hate people. You don't need to."

And he turns and walks out of the room. I hear him and Mom downstairs. Dad says something and I hear Mom's laugh. It's a sound I haven't heard in a long time. And hope creeps in.

Duge drops our CDs off at Real Tunes on Friday. The hands on the clock above the cash register have never moved more slowly. I bike home after work as fast as I can with the disks in my backpack. I knock on Gellie's door. Margie answers and tells me that Gellie's out with her mother, doing her modeling thing. I decide I just can't wait. I refuse to let Gellie or her mother stop me from having my dream. And maybe I like the fact that I have something over Gellie. She may control when and where and how much we get to practice, but I have the demo.

At home, I turn on my boom box and hold my breath. The sound of our two voices and two guitars is fuller on the CD than it is in my ears when we're playing together. And I hear what Mom and Duge mean when they say we blend. It's hard for me to tell who's who; we sound like two parts of the same voice. It's a little rough, but for our first recording it's pretty good. As I listen over and over again for the rest of the afternoon, it's more than good. We're great. I can't wait for John to hear it.

"When can you come over and hear the CD?" I say to Gellie on the phone when she finally calls me back.

"Soon," she says uncomfortably. Then in a whisper, "Mom's sort of on my case about spending any time at all on the music."

"Well, I need to give it to John. Tomorrow. And I want you to hear it, and I want to give it to him together. If you come by the store, we can play it for him on the store sound system."

"Tomorrow?" Gellie's pondering. "Yeah, that would work. I can come around eleven."

The next day, I'm so nervous, it's hard to concentrate on what John wants me to do. Every time the door opens, I look up, hoping it will be Gellie. I'm procrastinating, going through the bins of used CDs. I've pulled aside a couple of classic rock albums that Dad has on vinyl. His birthday's coming, and I want to give him an unforgettable gift.

John's in a terrible mood. He spilled grapefruit juice on his Powerbook and almost lost his screenplay. He kept saying, "Bollocks!" His friend Mark managed to get the screenplay onto a disk, but the actual computer won't boot up anymore, and he says he can't afford a new one. He's sitting behind the counter, wearing a blue-striped, slightly rumpled button-down shirt. His red hair is a little longer than usual, giving him an overall extra-forlorn look.

"Skivving off, are you?" he snaps at me.

"Just finding CDs for my dad," I mumble.

"That's not what I don't pay you for, is it? Here. Sticker this box."

So I put my CDs for Dad on the counter and retreat to the chair behind it with a box of guitar strings and a roll of yellow stickers.

The door opens, but it's not Gellie. It's Barbara. I pop up from behind the counter. She sees me and comes over with a note.

"Mom took Gellie to an audition," she says, handing it to me.

> Dear Randi,
> I'm really sorry. I had to go with Mom. Give John a CD without me. I'm really sorry!!
> Love,
> Gellie

I can't believe it. This is the most important thing we've ever done as a band, and Gellie's bagging out on me. Again. I slam the note down on the counter.

"Hey, don't be mad at Gellie," says Barbara, looking at me for the first time like I'm an actual person. "My mom can be a real piece of work. Margie and I have been talking about it." She leans in conspiratorially. "We think it's cool that you guys are trying to do this band thing. Don't give up on Gellie. Eventually, maybe Mom will find some other hobby, like collecting miniatures or something."

And she reaches across the counter and touches me on the shoulder, then leaves the store. I watch her go and want to ask questions about what else she and Margie think, but I'm too freaked out.

John comes around. "Who was that?"

"Gellie's sister. Gellie's auditioning for something." I don't know why I said that. John won't care. I guess I want someone to understand.

"Hmm," says John. "That Jellybean. She's really got something going on, doesn't she? Bit of an It Girl, her."

"Yeah," I say, though it comes out as a sort of croak.

John looks at me, puzzled. When I don't respond, he picks up the CDs I left on the counter. "These for your dad?"

I nod.

"Consider them part of your wages."

"Thanks," I say. It's time for me to go, and I feel the demo in my pocket. Suddenly it weighs a hundred pounds.

"Here," I say, handing it to him. "This is Gellie and me."

"Marv," says John, nodding and holding the demo as though it were an ancient and foreign artifact. "Yeah, I remember. I said I'd ring the powers that be for you."

☆ ☆ ☆

It's raining as I bike home. I can't believe what a letdown this whole demo thing is. I give myself a pep talk.

"Listen, Randi," I say to me. "You can't count on Gellie. She's busy with her modeling. You need to focus on *you*."

Hearing the demo makes me realize how pathetic my guitar playing is, even though I've been studying with John and practicing a lot. It seems to come so easily to Gellie. I have to get better, so I decide to do something about it. Dad owes me.

☆ ☆ ☆

"I demand a guitar lesson. Now," I say to Dad. It's Sunday, and he's watching the Cartoon Network. Old Warner Brothers cartoons are his favorite, and they're showing a special Daffy Duck marathon.

"Sweetheart, I'm really tired. I need my TV fix," he says. "Give me a couple of hours to watch TV and be completely irredeemable."

"How many more hours?" I persist.

"Until it's over," he says vaguely.

"In a few hours you're going to have to go to your gig," I remind him. OK, maybe I also kind of kick the bottom of the coffee table slightly. He switches to a simulcast of a Rolling Stones concert on TV. The Rolling Stones look like they're hanging together with duct tape and rubber cement. I can't believe anyone ever thought these guys were good-looking.

Dad's barely even my teacher anymore. Everything I've learned lately I learned from John. That and just listening to CDs. But I don't want to mention this, because what I really want is for Dad to sit down with me and show me stuff about the guitar that only he knows. And I really miss hearing him sing.

"How are your friends?" he adds absentmindedly, his eyes on the screen. "How's that Shawna?"

"OK, I guess," I say. "I'm not really hanging out with her. These days I mostly hang out with Gellie. Shawna's being kind of a jerk, actually."

"Hmm," he says. "Typical. Her parents got divorced, right?"

"Why do you always think if someone's mean, it's because her parents got divorced?"

"Well." He takes a drink of his soda. "It's tough on a kid when that happens."

He always says this. He's wrong. I know plenty of cool kids with divorced parents.

I storm outside into the scorching summer day. Now I'm angrier at Dad than I am at Gellie. Besides, she must be dying to hear the CD by now. I'm going to sit her down in her studio and force her to listen to it if it's the last thing I do. I look both ways and cross the street. The silver Audi is parked in front of Gellie's house, so I know Boo and Steve are there. No one answers when I knock, so I just go in. Mrs. Riddle is busting a gut about something.

"I hear Trevor is the only photographer *Sharpen You* is even touching," she says. "You *have* to get Trevor. What's the point of a photo shoot if the pictures won't be chosen by anyone except *Women's Day* and *Family Circle*? We're going for *Us* and *Entertainment Weekly* here. Or, at least, *People*."

Boo sighs dramatically and takes a huge drag off her cigarette, breaking Mr. Riddle's no-smoking-in-the-house rule. "Codified by a needlepoint sign," Barbara likes to say. That sign is hanging prominently in the living room right above Boo's head.

Steve smiles his huge piano-teeth smile. "June," he says, "we've done our own research, and I want to reassure you with every fiber of my partially divine being that Roberta is better than Trevor. She is the *best*. She's the one they've all been using. You've got to trust us here. The issue here is trust."

Boo echoes him in her gravelly voice as though he hasn't spoken. "THE ISSUE HERE IS TRUST. TRUST US, JUNE. WE'VE WORKED MIRACLES WITH YOUNG TALENT. MIRACLES. WHY SHOULD GELLIE BE ANY DIFFERENT?"

Gellie is sitting with her back to me, cross-legged on the hard upholstered sofa.

Mrs. Riddle looks up sharply and says, "Randi, what do you want?" It's more like a command than a question.

"Just to see if Gellie wants to . . . ," I want to say "play," but that makes me sound like I'm eight. But it *is* what I want to do. I want to go down to Gellie's studio and play guitar and rehearse our act in front of the mirror. I want to sit around talking about our big plans for Plastic Angel. I want to tell Gellie I gave a demo to John. I want us to listen to our CD together. And I want us to sing along to ourselves. There is nothing in the world more just plain *fun* than singing with Gellie, and I feel like if I don't get a taste of fun right about now, I'll die. But in my hesitation, Gellie turns around and looks at me apologetically.

"I have an interview in an hour with the Clairman *Observer*."

"They want to write a feature on Gellie as the youngest Clairmanite ever to garner such celebrity. They are titling the piece 'Young Star to Go Far,'" says Mrs. Riddle, looking at me through half-closed eyes. I imagine she's thinking, "I've won. Sucker!"

"IT'S NOT *VOGUE* OR *SEVENTEEN,* BUT IT'S A START," says Boo.

"I'll come back in about ten years, when it's over," I say and turn to go home.

"Randi," says Gellie. "Wait up." And she scrambles to her feet and follows me to the front door.

"I'm sorry I didn't meet you yesterday," she whispers.

I shrug.

"How's the demo? I'm dying to hear it."

And suddenly my anger is back. I don't tell her I have a copy with me in my bag. "It's good. You know where I live. Come listen to it. Anytime. Have your people call my people when you're available."

She nods. "Yeah. I'll call you. When all this dies down."

☆ ☆ ☆

Back in my house, Mom and Dad are fighting. I walk quickly to my bedroom, hang the CLOSED FOR GOOD sign on the door, and blast my Big Idea CD. But not before

I hear Dad say to Mom, "You're wrong about this, Madeleine. I *can* live with your moods. What I can't live with is your unwillingness to support me and my work."

"Well, then leave," she says. "If you can't see that support is about putting food on the table and making sure our daughter is clothed and educated, Guy, then I guess there's no support. But it's not me who's not being supportive. Or haven't you noticed which one of us has been faithfully depositing her paychecks into the joint account?"

I hear another door close, this one not so quietly. I look out the window and see Dad loading his little van with his guitar and gig bag. He comes back and forth a couple of times, first with a suitcase and then with the computer. I watch him drive away until I can't see his van anymore. I lie down on my bed, staring right at Emily Dickinson's picture. She has a half smile, kind of like Rhodie Becket's. Her head is cocked the way Gellie's is when she sings one of our songs. I whisper to Emily, "This whole world is crazy. This is *all* wrong." And I dream about Gellie and me flying away from Mrs. Riddle, from Boo and Steve, from Mom and Dad, from Clairman. About being a thing with feathers.

CHAPTER FOURTEEN

Solitaire

On my birthday, I get nearly everything I want. I go over to Aunt Izzie's, where Dad is staying, and watch *A Hard Day's Night* in the guest room, the only place in Aunt Izzie's apartment where you can find a TV. I've seen it, seriously, fourteen hundred times.

Mom loves *A Hard Day's Night,* too, and her favorite line comes next: It's when the Beatles are running alongside the train making faces at the grouchy old man and saying, "Mister, can we have our ball back?"

Dad and I don't look at each other or say anything at that part.

I'm trying not to think about the fact that Mom is home

alone on my birthday and we aren't all together for the first time in my whole life. Even when Dad had to be away for a tour, Mom and I always joined him wherever he was. Last year, we flew all the way to Puerto Vallarta, where Dad was the musical background for a business convention.

Earlier today, Mom and I had a birthday breakfast together. She brought a tray up to my bed: homemade Belgian waffles with strawberry syrup that she made last spring, a bowl of cut-up peaches, and a little pot of espresso with a silver pitcher of steamed frothy milk. She came in with a tray and squinched me over so she could sit next to me. She also gave me my presents: a new shirt to wear to school and a book called *Reviving Ophelia,* which is about how hard it is to be an adolescent girl. Like I need a book to tell me that.

Dad's been out of the house for two weeks. Eighteen days to be exact. Mom won't talk to me about it except to say it has nothing to do with me, about a million times a day. Dad says the same thing.

"I don't think it's forever, Randi. I couldn't live if I thought it was forever. But for today, yes, your mother and I are living separately."

☆ ☆ ☆

Dad gave me a new computer, a Powerbook, for my birthday. I keep changing the screen saver. Right now I've scanned in a photo of Mom, Dad, and me from last year at the restaurant we went to in Puerto Vallarta. Dad's in the middle, smiling his photo-shoot smile. He has his virgin piña colada in his right hand, which is behind my right ear. I am smiling, too, a very toothy grin. Mom has a closed-lipped smile. Dad's hand is holding her upper arm tightly.

I thought having my own computer would be the best present ever. I always hated having to share with Dad. But I have the feeling that Dad gave it to me to make up for the fact that he left and took his with him.

A few days later, as a belated birthday celebration, Aunt Izzie takes me out for lunch to this little French restaurant in Jintucket. We sit at a table on the street and order Caesar salads with tiny dishes of grapefruit sorbet.

"What a wonderful time of year for a birthday!" Aunt Izzie exclaims. "Early August always seems to me the time of year when the summer comes into its own, like a woman in her thirties. It becomes settled and mature and strong and beautiful. It's not so hot, and the bugs are finally tolerable."

I don't know what she's talking about. It's a million degrees outside today, and even in a tank top, I am sweating. But I just say "uh-huh" and eat my sorbet.

Aunt Izzie says, "Do you know what's going on with your parents?"

"Not really," I say. "I think maybe they just need a break from each other."

Aunt Izzie nods. She waves at some people passing by,

probably former No-Talent students. "I wouldn't worry, Randi."

"I'm not worried."

"I mean, they love each other very much. I don't think they'll get divorced."

The sorbet hurts the back of my throat with its tart coldness. "I'm not worried," I repeat.

Aunt Izzie continues, "It's probably a phase. They're both heading toward forty, and that's a really tough age. Especially for your dad. He's worried about his career these days, feeling inadequate. And your mother has always had trouble talking about what she *really* needs."

I hate it when Aunt Izzie talks this way.

"I think she's just mad because Dad's gone all the time," I say.

"Well, yes, sweetheart, but that's because it brings up stuff about *her* mother and father abandoning her when she was little."

"They didn't abandon her," I say angrily. "They gave her whatever she wanted. She ran away from home."

Aunt Izzie sighs. "They were never there for her. Trust me."

I've heard this a million times. I have no idea what it means — "they were never there for her" — and it pisses me off. The waitress comes by with the dessert tray, and I order the raspberry napoleon. Aunt Izzie gets crème brûlée flavored with Earl Grey tea.

"I wouldn't worry," she says again.

If I'm not supposed to be worried, why does she keep saying this?

☆ ☆ ☆

I don't want to talk to Gellie about my parents, so I don't. It's not hard to keep it a secret. She still hasn't even heard the demo.

Gellie's never home these days. It seems Boo and Steve call every other day with a new job. They shot a commercial for an acne product. In it, Gellie is covered with fake zits in the first half, then has miraculously clear skin in the second. Why she has to look so beautiful to play a kid with acne is beyond me. Though it has made me notice that *everyone* on TV is beautiful, even the ugly people. If you take an ugly TV person and set her down in a normal street, she wouldn't seem ugly; she'd seem normal. Just as TV adds ten pounds, it also adds ugliness, I guess. That's why Gellie is so completely obsessed with every hair on her head these days.

"My teeth look so yellow," she moans into the mirror. "This isn't working." She means her teeth-whitening strips, which she uses constantly, not just twice a day like you're supposed to. "See," she shows me her teeth. "Look at the yellow in the cracks in between."

It's so frustrating to be with Gellie and not get to practice or even really talk about the band. The unspoken rule — her mother's rule — seems to be that I can spend time with Gellie as long as the topics are centered on her and her modeling career. John hasn't called about the demo or mentioned it at work. It probably stinks. I should probably forget about it. Gellie has. And her fame as a model is growing. Everywhere we go in Clairman, Gellie gets recognized by moms and little kids.

"Such talent," cluck the moms.

"The girl from the pimple commercials!" shout the kids.

Today, we're at CVS. Gellie fills her shopping cart with gizmos: curling irons, hair dryers, serums to make your hair thicker. She gets three different women's magazines. We sit on the curb outside the dry cleaners, waiting for her mother to pick us up. Gellie reads aloud to me.

"Do you know that if you fidget enough, you burn two hundred extra calories a day?" she says, looking up from her magazine.

"No," I say.

"Well, it's true. That's probably why Shawna is so skinny."

"You're skinny."

"Yeah, but I'm getting this." She holds her upper arm like she's making a muscle. With her free hand, she pinches the skin between her shoulder and elbow.

"It's getting kind of flabby."

"You're whacked," I say.

Gellie nods. "I know. But it's just the way it is. Most models are whacked out about their bodies."

☆ ☆ ☆

In the middle of the night, I wake up from a dream. It's not a dream I can put into words, exactly. It's more of a tune.

I clearly hear a girl's voice singing. I hum it to myself. This has happened before, and I always think I'll remember the tune the next day, but I never do. This time I reach for my guitar and start to sing:

I finally get what my wings are for,
I finally get what my wings are for.

I expect more to come, but nothing does. I play these lines over and over for a while. I sing it to myself until I'm sure I won't forget it the next morning. And I don't.

☆ ☆ ☆

"Hey," I say when Gellie answers the phone the next morning.

"Hi, Randi."

"I've got the beginning of a song," I say. "Maybe we can try singing it sometime. I think it's going to be really good."

"You do?"

"Yeah."

Gellie is silent on the other end of the phone.

"So," I say finally. "Can you sneak over here and rehearse?"

I'm standing in front of the fridge with the door wide open, getting cooled off, even though Mom would yell if she saw me. I pull out a can of soda and an ice-cream sandwich, listening to Gellie's monologue about her incredibly busy and important life.

"I have to do a reading over the phone with the casting director for this movie my agents want me to go for. On Thursday, I have a voice lesson, and on Friday, we're down in New York for the Revlon shoot and then to meet a film director from California. The next time I'm free is probably a week from Wednesday."

"Fine," I say. "Put my name in your Palm Pilot. Please." I take an angry bite of ice-cream sandwich. Then I'm curious. "Are you psyched about the film director?"

"Sort of."

"What's it for, again?"

"This movie. I'm up for a small part in a story about animated dinosaurs who start a rock band."

"Who plays bass?" This is meant as a joke, but Gellie takes me seriously.

"I think the stegosaurus, but I'm not really sure."

OK, this is beyond ridiculous. I blurt out, "Why would you want to be in this inane movie?"

The line is so quiet, I wonder if she's hung up on me. Then she says, "I don't."

"So don't," I say, feeling a surge of hope.

"I have to go do a photo shoot in Boston tomorrow for *Little Miss* magazine," says Gellie, ignoring what I just said. "Will you come?"

I want to say no way. But honestly, I miss Gellie. I'll take what I can get. So I'll play by Mrs. Riddle's rules. I say yes.

Mom comes to my door later that day in between treating patients. "Honey, where did I leave my glasses?"

"Beats me," I say, without even looking up from my Powerbook. I've gotten really good at solitaire. I have the top score, in my own Powerbook, anyway. Mom has rationed my solitaire time to no more than a half hour a day. Not that she ever bothers to check to see what I'm doing on my computer. For all she knows, I could be having an online affair with a pervert.

"I wish your father had never bought you that computer," Mom says.

"Hmm," I say.

"I didn't spend my hard-earned money on Clairman Country Day so you could be a video-game expert," she continues.

"So send me to public school," I say, not looking up. "I don't care."

"Well, I do. And so would you if you paid any attention."

She's right. I know my mom really cares about me. But before I can say anything, she's disappeared from my doorway. A few minutes later, I hear her crying. I feel a sudden shock, like someone's broken a window. And like my chest is full of the broken glass.

CHAPTER FIFTEEN

A Short Leash

It's still summer, but the very first red and orange leaves are showing. They mean school isn't far off, and I am not ready for school to start. I don't want to leave Real Tunes. I thought by the end of the summer I'd be a rock and roller and have a new identity. Instead, I'm just going to revert to being Boring Randi.

Gellie's passion for Plastic Angel is fading. She still hasn't heard our demo CD, not that I've even mentioned it recently. I know I'm not allowed to talk about the band in front of Mrs. Riddle, so when I climb into the silver Volvo with Gellie to go to her photo shoot, we just sing along to the Broadway-musical soundtracks Mrs. Riddle plays. This, she approves of.

I look out the window. We're passing a rest stop. Lately, if I don't have my guitar and a song in my head, all I can think about is Mom and Dad. I imagine solving the problem: how Dad could have his career and stay home with Mom and me at the same time. If he had a really big hit. If he taught guitar lessons at Real Tunes. If he worked at Starbucks. If Mom quit acupuncture and I quit school and we just traveled with him all the time . . .

"Smile, *bella*. Oh, so *bella*! That's it! Work it, girlfriend, work it!" The photographer glides around the room like a swan. I never knew how graceful you had to be to take pictures. But I also never knew how boring it was to watch someone be photographed over and over, just moving around in the space of a couple of feet. Gellie looks tired of smiling. If I'm bored, I can't imagine how she must feel.

I leave to get a bag of potato chips from the vending machine, and on my way back, I hear Boo and Steve talking to Seymour Simpson, the editor of *Little Miss* magazine.

"The mother is, you know, a little hard to take," Steve is saying. "But we're working with her."

Boo repeats, "WE'RE ABLE TO WORK WITH HER."

I stand completely still. They're on the other side of the

door from me now. Mrs. Riddle's in the front, behind the photographer's shoulder, and out of earshot.

Mr. Simpson sighs. "Yeah, with kids who start this young, it's always a race to see which goes first, the body or the mind. This one's lasted a pretty long time. Usually, they either get too puffy or acne-covered or end up in the psych ward. The parent's crucial. If the parent's half sane, there's a little more longevity for the kid's career."

"And this kid's pretty compliant," says Steve. "She goes where we tell her to go. She does what we want her to do."

Seymour Simpson chuckles. "Wait'll she gets a boyfriend. It'll be all over then."

"OH, WE'VE TOLD THE MOM TO KEEP HER ON A SHORT LEASH," Boo assures him.

"That's the way it's got to be if she wants to go anywhere," says Seymour Simpson.

I crumple the bag of chips and come through the doorway. Boo and Steve and Seymour look my way and then go back to their conversation. They don't even care that I might have heard them, which makes me almost as angry as all the things they've been saying. Don't they get that I'm a spy? Don't they care that I could convince Gellie to quit this stupid modeling thing by telling her what they said, about how she'd end up in a psych ward?

But then I see her in front of the camera. She's wearing a necklace and fake diamond earrings the photographer gave her. "Adds sparkle!" he told her. "You shine like a lit-tle star!"

And I wonder, even if I did tell her what they said, would she be willing to let this go? Would she give this up?

How I wonder what you are, Gellie Riddle.

I will not let Gellie be kept on a short leash. So on the way home, I loudly ask Gellie if she wants to come over to practice. Mrs. Riddle freaks. "Gellie, I'm not going to watch the years I've put into you go down the toilet."

"I don't think our music is . . . toilet-worthy," I say, realizing immediately that saying our music isn't toilet-worthy could be taken to mean our music sucks so bad it isn't even worthy of being in the toilet. I can never find the right comeback when Mrs. Riddle says things that I dis-agree with. I'm always coming up with the best responses when I'm lying in bed at night trying to fall asleep.

Gellie shoots me a warning look.

"If you think you're going anywhere with a guitar and a couple of pop songs, you're sorely mistaken. Do you know how many people spend their whole lives banging their heads against the wall trying to break into the music business? You have to stick to your true talent, Gellie. I can help you with that, darling. I've been there. I know how to play the game. I know the rules."

I think of Dad. How he plays gig after gig, even though it doesn't look like he's going to get famous anytime soon.

He's not playing any game. He's just doing what he really loves. Sometimes it must feel like he's banging his head against the wall. But he goes out and plays his shows just the same.

"Why don't *we* make the rules?" I mutter under my breath.

Gellie looks at me sideways and then looks quickly away, out the window. And I look out mine. I count birds on the telephone wires. Forty-seven of them by the time the car pulls into my driveway. Dad's van is there for the first time in weeks.

"Bye," I say and run toward the door.

"Hey, Randi," says Gellie out the window, "I wanted to tell you something."

"Tell me later," I shout over my shoulder.

☆ ☆ ☆

Inside, it's as if the temperature dropped twenty degrees. Mom has the freezer open and is making her health-food-juice Popsicles with the ice tray. She doesn't turn to look at me when I come in. Her face is red and blotchy and her mouth is white. Dad comes down the stairs with a box full of his stuff. He looks really tired. He sees me and says, "Hi, Glory." He catches my eye but looks away.

His box slips and falls to the floor with a crash. Outside, the squirrels that were foraging for acorns skitter back up the trees, as if they heard the noise in our house. Dad curses and leans over to pick up his things. I want to help but something stops me. I want to speak, but the words are stuck in my throat and everything I think of to say seems babyish and stupid. The cats are fighting in the next room, which usually makes us all laugh, but now we ignore it.

Mom sniffles. I want to put my hand on her shoulder or something, but maybe that would make Dad think I'm on her side. I don't know what to do, so I just go up to my bedroom. On the way, I hear Mom say, "This is so unfair to her."

Dad sighs and says, "This isn't about her, Madeleine. It's about us. When you're ready to talk about *us*, then we'll have something to talk about."

"And when you're ready to acknowledge that she is part of us, then I'll believe we have something to talk about."

A door slams downstairs. I slam my door, too. Our house is a symphony of slamming doors. I try to sign on to my new computer, but the system doesn't respond. I try to print out a copy of the photo of Gellie and me that Duge e-mailed me yesterday, but my computer isn't compatible with the old printer Mom gave me. It's only compatible with the printer Dad took. I'm so mad, I want to throw the Powerbook against the wall and watch it break. Instead, I leave it sitting cockeyed on top of a stack of old papers and magazines. It blinks at me. I turn my back on it and pick up my guitar. I play a few chords and promptly break a string. I look up at the poster of Rhodie Becket. She looks like she's mocking me now. Not like we're sharing a joke.

There's a knock on my door.

"Go away," I say. Gellie comes in. She's wearing this little knit hat her mother made her. Her T-shirt rides up and shows her skinny stomach. I can't tell if she's trying to be sexy or just outgrowing her clothes.

"Hey," she says solemnly. "Where's your Dad going this time?"

"Oh, you know," I say. "On some tour."

"I finally have a little time to listen to the CD," she says, looking at her watch. "So I thought I'd come by."

That does it.

"Well, I'm about to go out," I say. "I'm meeting Essie and Shawna at the mall. Sorry."

Gellie looks surprised. "I thought you said we needed to practice. Can't you call them and reschedule?"

"Oh, fine, when it's my plans, I'm supposed to reschedule. But when it's you and your precious career, nothing is more sacred. Forget it, Gellie. Go home and pluck your eyebrows or something."

I have a fiery rush through my body and it makes me feel better for a second. Then I feel horrible. I hear Gellie charge down the stairs, and for a second, I just sit on the bed, watching my red lava lamp and hating her, hating my parents, hating everyone. I go to the window and watch her start to cross the street, back to her house, back to the place where she has to be beautiful, has to have unfrizzy hair, has to have white teeth, has to be flab-free. And I hate being by myself about ten times more than I hate anyone else.

"Hey," I shout, opening the window. "Come back! I'll play you the demo."

Gellie turns and glares up at me, shielding her eyes with her hand. She looks at me for a long time. Then she says, "I'll be right up. I just have to get something." And she disappears into her house.

☆ ☆ ☆

"What'd you do about Shawna and Essie?" she asks, arranging herself on my bed a few minutes later.

"Let them wait," I say. I put the CD in my boom box and press PLAY. Nothing happens. I check the plug. It's in the wall. I press PLAY again. The CD player starts to spin, but then it stops. It dies. I start to cry and I can't stop.

"Nothing works today!" I say. "Everything is broken! And I have no idea if you even want to be in this stupid band."

I have my hands over my face, wet with tears. I don't hear anything for a while. Then Gellie says, very gently, "Open your eyes."

I look up and there's a little wrapped package on my desk, next to my cockeyed computer.

As I unwrap it, Gellie says, "I felt like you needed this. Because, you know, you have a lot going on. You're supposed to wind it up and put it on top of your boom box, your computer, anything that's not working. The angel is supposed to fix it. Maybe it'll work on other stuff, too. I've been wanting to give you one since we never got to go to the mall that time after I found the angel in my closet."

She winds it up and puts it on top of my boom box. We sit on the bed together, watching its wings flap back and forth mechanically. I feel like I can breathe again for the first time in weeks. A breeze blows through the window I left open.

"What did you think of that photo shoot, anyway?" I finally say.

"Boring," says Gellie. "My feet hurt."

I look out the window and hear a rising hum of summer insects. It sounds like my guitar pick scratching up the bass string.

"My dad moved out," I say. It sounds like another person's voice, not my own. "He's not really on tour. He's not living here anymore."

"What?"

"Yeah." I exhale. "About three weeks ago. He's living with Aunt Izzie."

"That sucks" is all Gellie says. But somehow, it's enough.

"Yup," I say. Gellie puts her hand on my arm and holds it there. Not squeezing, not limp, either. Firm and present. It acts sort of like a truth serum.

"Martin Forrest kissed me," I blurt out. "At that party of Essie's after you left. I thought my life would be excellent if I got kissed by a cute boy, and Martin is cute enough. But the kiss was nothing like what I imagined kissing would be."

Gellie's silent, and I feel guilty again for dumping her at the party. But then she just asks, "What was it like?"

"Wet."

"Oh," says Gellie. I could see she is sort of uncomfortable — and did I detect a bit of jealousy? But she quickly changes the subject. "That night at the party, while you were dancing with Martin, Shawna Gilbert said she was surprised to see me there because she'd always thought I was in sixth grade. She said, 'No offense. When you're forty, you'll be glad you look so young.' Then she smiled pseudo sweetly and looked me up and down like she couldn't believe how dumb my clothes were."

"She's a snob and a jerk," I say. "She knows perfectly well you're in our grade."

"She said she would look for someone short for me to dance with."

"You could've danced with Duge," I say.

"And what exactly would that have accomplished? That would just prove everyone's point. Shawna would say two losers like us belong together." She winds up the plastic angel again, and we watch it vibrate. "Sometimes I want a place-saver boyfriend," she continues. "Or even just to be like Margie and have a Not Boyfriend like Jeremy. To make everyone think I'm . . . normal."

"Yeah," I say. "That's what I was thinking, too. That's why I kissed Martin. But it didn't work. I should've just gone home with you that night."

Gellie smiles and shrugs, and I know I'm forgiven. "Face it, Randi. We're never going to be normal. We're different."

"But you *like* being different. Don't you? You like being The Face of Clairman. You like being Your Goddessness."

"Yeah, I do. I admit it. But you know how I feel after a competition?"

"Like a Goddess?"

"Well, at first, yeah. I feel all glowy and shiny and warm. But the next morning, I feel sort of sick. Like when you eat too much chocolate or something. I feel gross."

"Hmm," I say. "So quit. Tell your mother you don't want to do it anymore."

Gellie shakes her head. "Maybe someday," she says. "I don't know. And I don't know what *Mom* would do if I weren't doing this."

Gellie gets up and presses PLAY. This time the room fills with the sounds we made a few weeks ago, though it seems like years ago now. The first song is "Clairman Town." We listen to the entire demo together, noticing the places where we need to improve, but mostly we just gloat about how great we sound.

"You know what?" says Gellie.

"What?"

"This is what I love best. When we're singing together, I don't care what anyone says about me, ever. Not even Shawna."

"Who cares about Shawna?" I say, though it's not quite true. I do care about Shawna. I just *wish* I didn't. But maybe if I say strong things like that, I'll make them real.

Ideas can turn into something outside of yourself and get a life of their own.

The thing is I feel as though I've been forever trying to play by rules I don't even get but people like Shawna instinctively seem to know. And even if I could somehow figure them out, all that would happen is that I'd end up being popular with girls who'd ultimately bore me to death.

"When we go back to school this year, I'm not going to try to be friends with The Tribe anymore," I say. "If they want to be friends with me, fine. But I'm not going to play their game anymore. I have enough friends, real friends. You, Duge, John. I'm done trying to be popular."

After a minute, Gellie says, "Maybe I could be done trying to be famous. Maybe we can just have a big truce and say we've had enough of this trying to get to the next level. Randi is almost popular and that's enough. Gellie is almost famous and that's enough. From now on, we're going to just be us. We're going to be loyal to ourselves and Plastic Angel. We're going to make our own rules."

I want to hug Gellie. Instead I nod vigorously and say, "Deal."

She gets up to go. "I'm leaving the angel with you. So you know that even when I'm doing modeling stuff, I'm really here. The angel is my place saver. And who knows — maybe it'll fix what's broken."

"Thanks," I say. "I can use it today."

CHAPTER SIXTEEN

Gellie's Big Break

I am finishing a song. Just as I come up with the last line, the phone rings.

"Is Randi there?" The voice is familiar, with a British accent.

"This is Randi."

"Well, Miss Rankin, this is your agent, or have you forgotten the little people already, now that you're a professional musician?"

"What do you mean?" I say, though I know already. I don't know which to be more excited about — that John has just called me or that we might have a gig.

"Next Friday night at ten o'clock you and Gellie Riddle

are scheduled to perform as Plastic Angel at May Day Café in West Jintucket," beeps John in a monotone as if he's an android. "Payment shall be as follows: pass-the-hat and a free dinner. Do you accept these wages?"

"I accept!" I yell. "Oh, my God! I accept! Thank you thank you thank you!"

"You're welcome you're welcome you're welcome!" John laughs. "Just give me a quarter of the turkey sandwich they feed you. And remember me when you're famous."

☆ ☆ ☆

I dash out the front door and run across the road to Gellie's. I realize as I'm running that next Friday is Dad's birthday. I have fantasies about him celebrating at May Day Café, proudly watching his only child perform her own songs — and maybe some of his — for the first time.

Then my heart sinks. The silver Audi is in the driveway. I try to pull the sliding glass door open, but it's been locked. I see Boo and Steve and Gellie and Mrs. Riddle all inside. They turn to look at me, and Gellie opens the door. She looks beautiful. Her hair is piled on top of her head, and she's wearing a tank top we bought together at Hillary's Hipper.

"Randi," says Gellie seriously, sliding open the door. "I have some big news."

"So do I," I say.

"I got the part."

"What part?"

"Stella. In the dinosaur movie. Remember?"

"It's the break of a lifetime!" hoots Steve. "It's big-time. It's really big-time."

"It's a career maker," sings Mrs. Riddle.

"It's a hundred and fifty thousand dollars," says Gellie evenly, looking me in the eye.

"Wow," I say. "Wow." A hundred and fifty thousand dollars is the number Dad's always joking about. "I'm going to write a hit song and make a hundred and fifty *thousand* dollars!" he'll crow.

"THEY'RE FLYING HER OUT TO HOLLYWOOD NEXT WEEK!" says Boo, jumping up and down like a yappy little dog. "I TOLD YOU WE'D COME THROUGH FOR YOU, I TOLD YOU! DIDN'T I TELL YOU, JUNE?"

What am I supposed to do now? Tell them all about our first gig? Try to convince everyone that maybe somehow Gellie and I will pull in a hundred and fifty thousand dollars in pass-the-hat at May Day Café — and get laughed out of the Riddle house?

I take a deep breath and announce what I was going to say. "We got a gig. May Day Café. Next Friday."

"Gellie will be in California by then," says Mrs. Riddle quickly. "Besides, she doesn't have a guitar anymore. I sent it off to the Salvation Army this morning."

"That was Margie's guitar!" Gellie cries.

"She never played it," retorts Mrs. Riddle.

"Yeah, Mom, but *I* did!" I've never heard Gellie talk back to her mother. It makes me a little hopeful.

"I don't understand what's gotten into you lately. You've always been a good girl. You were always as happy as the day is long," Mrs. Riddle says, trying but failing to contain her anger. "What happened?"

"She is a good girl," I yell. "She's perfect, in fact! She's beautiful, smart, and really talented. But she deserves to live her own life! She deserves to get to make mistakes!"

"Randi, we're having a family moment." Mrs. Riddle points to the sliding glass door.

Boo and Steve are standing awkwardly behind the couch now. I look at Gellie, hoping she'll leave with me. But she's cowering now. She's a coward. All my doubts about her come back. She's going to fly off to California and leave me in the dust. I spin around and stomp out of the house. I'm halfway down her driveway when I realize she's following me. I can hear her feet.

"All right," she says when she's caught up to me. "You're right. I need to start playing by my own rules."

"That means you'll have to break some of theirs," I snap, not breaking my stride.

"I just did," she says. "I'm not taking the part. I told them."

"You're not taking the part? But it's a lot of money." I stop halfway down her driveway.

"No. It would be stupid to take the part. I thought about how I'd feel, being in California away from home. Being in a movie about dinosaurs in a rock band. That's just not how I want to spend my time."

I don't know what to say. Which is fine, because she keeps talking. I stop walking and listen.

"I want to be singing our songs. I want to *sing*. I want to say what *I* want to say, not some stupid words some idiot wrote for me to say, not what my mom wants me to say."

"What do you want to say?" I ask, though it comes out as more of a croak.

"That I'll stand up straight, stand up tall, and look everyone in the eye!" Gellie says fiercely. "That I could fly if I wanted to."

"Wings," I murmur.

"Yeah," Gellie says. "Wings. And I want to live by my own rules, like we always say."

"Well," I say, smiling. "If you want to, you will."

"And besides," says Gellie seriously, "you're going through a lot right now. With your parents and all. Maybe you need me around."

But just then the silver Audi pulls up beside us and screeches to a halt. The door flies open, and Mrs. Riddle leans out of the backseat and grabs Gellie before she knows what's happening. The car smokes off to the end of the driveway and turns left, toward Abigail Adams Boulevard, toward the airport.

CHAPTER SEVENTEEN

Powerbook for a Gibson

"What do you mean Gellie's been abducted?" shouts Barbara. "Who abducted her?"

"Your mother," I shout back. I'm standing on the side of the tennis court. Barbara is in the quarterfinals of the Clairman Country Club annual Labor Day tournament. She's winning easily, which is why I don't feel so bad telling her in the middle of a game that her sister's been kidnapped.

"So what else is new?" She hits the ball down the line, and her opponent lunges fruitlessly for it. Barbara trots over to me and wipes her forehead with a towel. "No, seriously, tell me what you're talking about."

"Gellie got the role in the dinosaur movie," I say slowly. "She doesn't want to take it. It would mean she'd have to go to Hollywood for the rest of the summer and miss the beginning of school. Plus, our first gig," I add as though it's an afterthought.

Barbara rolls her eyes. "How is this different from any other year? Gellie's gone away before. What's the big deal?"

I stop to think about this. "It's different," I say. "Gellie's different. And, anyway, what does it matter? She doesn't want to go this time. Why isn't that enough? Why doesn't she get to decide whether or not she takes this role?"

Barbara takes a long drink of water and wipes off the grip of her racquet. "Hang on," she says. "I'm almost finished with my match."

She goes back on the court. I sit down and watch. Duge comes over the hill and joins me on the bench alongside the court.

"I heard," he says.

"How did you hear?" I say, incredulous. How could he have heard? I didn't tell anyone but Barbara, and she hasn't left the tennis court since I told her.

"It doesn't matter," he says. He puts his hand on my shoulder. "Don't worry. You'll get through it. I'll be your friend through the hardest part. I know you feel alone and abandoned, but that's just an illusion. People come and go from your life, and you learn to live without them. Or at least in a new and different way."

"What are you talking about?" I say hotly. "Some people

you just can't replace. Besides. She's not gone forever. She's going to figure out a way to get out of this, I'm sure. They can't force her to perform like a trained monkey."

Now Duge looks confused. "What are *you* talking about?"

"Gellie's abduction," I say, shaking him by the shoulders.

"Oh," says Duge. He looks down at his hands, folded between his knees.

"What were you talking about?"

"Umm," says Duge. "Your parents."

"Who told you about my parents?"

"Gellie was abducted?"

☆ ☆ ☆

"I think calling it an abduction is an overstatement," says Barbara when I've told her and Duge the whole story. "They can't have gone far. Today's the day Margie gets back from her week in Montreal, and we're all having family dinner at seven o'clock. I can't believe Mom would've taken off to California. They probably just took Gellie around the block and tried to convince her to take the role."

"OK," says Duge. "If that's true, that buys us a little time. But we still haven't figured out how to keep them from taking Gellie to California. And how to get Randi and Gellie to their gig next Friday. And how to get Gellie's guitar out of the Salvation Army."

"If it even *is* at the Salvation Army," I moan. "I can't believe she'd give away Gellie's guitar."

"Margie's guitar," Barbara corrects me. "And Margie's going to be so mad. Not that she ever plays, but for a Socialist, she's very into her own property. She's going to have a fit."

"Isn't there somewhere you two can hole up?" says Duge. "Just for a week or so?"

I feel a rush. This would be really dangerous. But I imagine how I would feel if Gellie went to California.

"Well," I say, "Aunt Izzie's. But she's in New Mexico. I doubt we could get there and back in time for the gig."

"I thought she lived in Jintucket," says Duge.

"Only for part of the year," I say. "And now she's in Taos."

"So who's in her apartment now?" says Duge with a sly grin.

I am lying on my bed in the dark, staring at the stars on the ceiling, waiting for the doors to stop opening and closing, which will mean Mom's finally in bed. I have my old Snoopy red cloth suitcase with the broken zipper opened next to me on my bed. I've just put in the essentials: clothes for the gig, my L.L.Bean toiletries case, a change of guitar strings, and the money I got from selling my computer.

I knew exactly what I could get for the Powerbook because I checked it out on eBay. I also knew exactly who wanted it.

John looked up the second I came in with it. "Hey, there, future rock girl," he said. He was sitting on a stool behind the counter with his red high-tops propped up so he could tilt back and forth. He had a clipboard on his lap and the newest copy of *Rolling Stone*. "Ready for your big gig?"

"Depends," I said. "Would you buy my computer?"

John looked at me. "Your computer," he repeated.

"Yeah," I said. "I need the money." What was the point of beating around the bush?

He sighed. "How much do you want for it, Randi?"

I looked over the aisles of CDs to the instruments hanging on the wall and all the white price tags dangling from the necks of the guitars. There was a whole assortment: four electrics, two acoustics, and a bass. Among the electrics were two Ibanez, a used Fender, and a Les Paul. There was an ugly white acoustic Yamaha. My eyes skipped over these and fixed on a vintage Gibson acoustic, three-quarter size, walnut colored. The price tag said $500.

"Five hundred dollars," I said.

"For a new Powerbook?" he said. "Show me."

I pulled it out of my knapsack. It was white, almost silver. I opened it up and turned it on. Its little white apple glowed like ET's heart. The photo of me and my parents filled the screen.

"It's fully loaded," I said. "Plus, it's got all sorts of games. Solitaire's my favorite."

John was scrolling through my files. He looked up at me. "Why are you doing this, Miss Rankin?"

I looked at the screen. You couldn't see my family anymore because he had the menu covering us, but I focused on Dad's hand holding the virgin piña colada. "I need a new guitar," I said. "Plus, I'm not really such a computer kind of person, I've decided."

"In the twenty-first century, that's like saying, 'I'm not much for automobiles,'" said John, but he was reaching in his pocket and counting out some cash. "Here. Take this. I've added some for the fact that it's fully loaded."

He handed me thirty-two twenty-dollar bills. I started to protest, but he put up his hands.

"Don't ever argue when someone gives you too much money. Trust me on that. Now. Let's get you a guitar."

The Gibson had an amber pick guard and matching tuning machines. It was worn away on the top and bottom of the sound hole, where its previous owner had left strum marks. It didn't matter.

"Where'd you get this one?" I asked John.

John smiled. "If I tell you, you won't believe me."

"Why wouldn't I believe you?"

"Because it belonged to Rhodie Becket of The Big Idea."

"You're right. I don't believe you."

John shrugged. "Fine. I'll prove it." And he picked up the telephone, dialed a few numbers, and handed it to me. I pushed it back at him as though it had the plague.

John sighed. "Oh, hey, Rhodie, please? Yeah, Rhodie — John here. Will you kindly tell my customer slash coworker what exactly you brought in to hock last week?"

John nodded at me and handed me the phone. I took it gingerly.

"Hello?" I said.

The voice is familiar, female, tough.

"Hey, kid. It's my guitar. I hocked it because our van needed a new transmission. It's a great guitar, but honestly it needs a lot of work. Now give the phone back to John."

"Um, thanks," I said into the phone.

John laughed. "Thanks, Rhodie. See you. You're coming down to the show? Great. I'll buy you a twig tea."

He laughed some more and hung up.

"That wasn't really Rhodie," I said, though I knew it was, and John knew I knew it was, too. "What show, uh, were you talking about, anyway?"

"Whose do you think? My new artists', who are playing next Friday at the May Day Café, *naturally*," said John, sorting through a box of multicolored flat picks. "So. Do you want it?"

I nodded. Rhodie Becket's guitar! Gellie was going to flip!

He pulled the guitar off the wall and handed it to me. I put my hands all over it, feeling a little guilty and self-conscious, like I was making out with it or something. It had the curves I always thought a guitar should have. The wood was the same color on the face as it was on the back, except that around the sound hole, it turned from brunette to blonde. I strummed a chord. I looked up at John, and he saw the anguish in my face.

"Yeah, it does sound a bit crap," said John, taking the guitar. "Well, that's why Rhodie is only selling it for five hundred dollars. No worries. 'Ang on." And he stuck a hex wrench into the belly of the guitar and poked around, every now and then holding the neck up and viewing the guitar by looking down it from the head where the tuning pegs are. He closed one eye and stuck his tongue out of the side of his mouth. I could hear him breathe. Finally, he handed the guitar back to me and said, "Here, try this."

I struck a chord and the action was much lower now, the guitar much easier to play. I played single notes at the open string and the octave for each string. I'm not the world's greatest guitar player, but it sounded pretty good to me.

"Thanks," I said.

"Don't mention it. Least I can do, you working for me all these weeks on the cheap."

John came around the counter and took the Gibson from me. He started singing one of our songs.

When I let you into my closet.

He looked into my eyes as he sang, but when I stared straight back, he closed his eyes and started clowning.

When I sold you this Gibson guitar
I already knew that you were a star.

"So you'll be at the gig Friday, right?" said John.

"Of course," I said, my heart hammering.

"Well, here, then." He reached into his pocket and pulled out another twenty. "Consider this an advance. I'm sure you'll make at least that much at May Day Café. And I'll be there to help out. Corral the autograph hounds and all that."

"You're going to be there?" I said.

"Wouldn't miss it for the world."

I hope Gellie and I don't, either. I check the clock; it's midnight. I haven't heard anything from Mom's room for a few minutes, so I get up and sneak out of the house. I cross the street with a guitar in each hand and my Snoopy suitcase under one arm. There's a full moon to light the way up Gellie's driveway. Now I'm standing under her window. I look at my watch. 12:07.

"Gellie," I whisper as loudly as I can. The curtains are drawn, and I can't see any movement through them. So I start whistling the newest song Gellie and I have been working on together. It doesn't have a name yet, and we haven't finished writing all the words, but there's this one part that goes, "Why don't you make the rules? / Why don't you make the rules?"

Gellie appears in the window. She is in her PJs: a T-shirt and yoga pants. When she sees me standing there, her eyes open very wide.

"Randi," she hisses, "what are you doing here?"

"Trying to convince you to blow this pop joint," I say. That's a Johnism. I really have no idea what a pop joint is. I'm not sure Gellie's house qualifies.

"What?" says Gellie.

"We're running away," I say.

"Are you crazy?" says Gellie. But her face is shining.

"I know where we can go," I say. "You only need your toothbrush and all the cash you can find. And bring the velvet shirt," I say as an afterthought. Velvet shirts are incredibly useful. They're nice for performing in and also very warm. I rub my upper arms; it's cool for late August, and I am praying that Mercury, the god of runaways, will look down benevolently upon us. Gellie's face disappears. For a few minutes I stand in the backyard, looking around. It hadn't occurred to me till now that maybe midnight was too early to carry out this plan, that Gellie's household might not be entirely asleep. But just as I start to walk around the house to check on what other lights might be on, I hear her window slide open, and there is Gellie with a tiny backpack on.

"Ready," she says grinning. "Where are we going?"

"Izzie's," I say. "You'll have to carry this." And I hand her the second guitar.

She looks at me.

"For you," I say. "It's a Gibson."

CHAPTER EIGHTEEN

The Bridge

The car thing was awful, Randi."

This is the first thing Gellie says for several minutes.

As soon as we got out of earshot of our two houses, she put down her new guitar and threw her arms around me.

"Thank you," she whispered. "I don't know how you got me this. I don't know what I ever did to deserve a friend like you. I don't feel worthy. But thank you, anyway."

I didn't tell her that I'd sold my computer. That can wait. Instead I said, "It's what friends do. You would've done the same for me."

She smiled and said, "If you needed me to, I would. I just need to figure out what the equivalent is."

"The equivalent?"

"To saving me."

"Hmm," I said. "Maybe you already have."

Now, we are almost to the river. The moon has been guiding us, even giving us enough light to make our way along the dark two-lane road. Once a car swerved as its headlights caught the two of us coming around a bend. We had to hug our guitars close to our chests to be as narrow as possible. Chain Bridge will take us over the Jintucket River. The road leading up to it runs between banks that are very steep and high. If a car were to come too close to us, there would be nowhere to go. We'd be squashed into the bank. So Gellie and I walk one in front of the other, making communication hard.

Gellie is in back of me. It's easier to hear what she says than to answer, and I'm glad to hear her say something. I was beginning to worry that her silence meant she was having second thoughts.

"Where did they take you?" I ask.

"I don't know," she says. "It was sort of like a mob movie. They drove me around and around the block, all of them talking at once, trying to convince me to do the dinosaur thing. The veins in all of their necks got all bulgy and purple. It became surreal after a while. I started to cry and finally said I'd do it. That's when they brought me home. By the time we got back, Dad and Margie had already gotten home and were pretty puzzled because Mom wasn't there cooking dinner. We ended up ordering out pizza for Margie's first night home from Montreal, which is, of course, very un-Riddle-like."

I think about how Barbara drove me all the way to Real Tunes to get the guitar and then home again. That was pretty un-Riddle-like, too.

"Barbara really cares about you, you know," I say.

Gellie responds quietly, "Yeah, I know. Margie does, too. She came into my room last night after everyone was in bed and said, 'You really can decide not to do this, you know.'"

"What did you say to her?"

"I said, 'How? I'm only thirteen. I'm an indentured servant.' Margie said that was offensive. But then she said she would think about it and help me however she could."

We walk on. The neat houses line the road. Very few lights are on in the windows by now, and it seems as if the whole town is asleep.

"I guess," says Gellie after a while, "I was afraid of letting Mom down. She's worked so hard, all for me. And even though it's her dream and maybe not so much mine . . . I still kind of like parts of being a model. I like getting attention. I like being special. I'm scared I'll lose that."

I think about this. "That's funny," I say finally. "I think maybe I'm scared of the same thing, that if I don't have something that makes me special, I'll be boring. That I'll never be popular."

"But you are popular! Everybody likes you!" says Gellie.

"Why do you think that?"

"Because it's true! Everyone loves you! You're like the nicest person in the school."

"I'm 'nice'? What kind of a word is that? No one wants to be just *nice*."

"All right, then. You're funny, and fun, and talented. And you're just . . . you. You're a Goddess. Your Randiness. Your Angelness."

"Well," I say, giggling in the dark. "Same to you."

☆ ☆ ☆

We are now at Chain Bridge, where there's a pedestrian sidewalk, and we're able to walk side by side.

"How much farther to Izzie's?"

I look at my watch. It's one-thirty. "Not more than a half hour," I say.

"Does she know we're coming?"

"Well, I'm sure she *knows*," I start. "In some kind of deep, you know, *knowing* way. But I didn't exactly talk to her."

"What do you mean?" says Gellie, showing her first hint of anxiety all night.

"I left a message on her answering machine saying we were having a gig on Friday, but I don't think she'll be able to come, being that she went back to Taos."

"She's in Taos?"

"Uh-huh."

"And all you said on her answering machine was we have a gig next Friday?"

"Yup."

"That's all you said?"

"Yeah, that and something about the full moon being a good time for taking a walk," I say, looking at the moon over the Jintucket. "But it's OK. I know for a fact that she always leaves her downstairs window unlocked; the one above the maple tree."

"Randi!" Gellie stops and puts down her guitar. I take the opportunity to do the same. I sit on its hard case and pull out the little bottle of water I'd stuck in my bag. I hand some to Gellie, but she waves it off angrily.

"What?" I say.

"You mean we're going to stay in an empty apartment?"

I take a long drink. "You would prefer we stay in a full apartment and run the risk of Boo and Steve and your mom coming to get you before our gig?" I say. It's begun to get a little chilly, and I'm glad I brought an extra long-sleeved shirt. Gellie's shivering. She puts on her velvet shirt. We sit on our guitar cases and have a snack. I give her some Sour Dudes, the green apples and the cherries. I eat the watermelon ones.

After a while, I say, "Of course, Dad might be there."

Gellie is silent. I am expecting her to yell at me again, because if Dad's there, we're busted. But instead she says, "Why did your parents split up?"

"They didn't split up. They're just not living in the same place right now. They're kind of mad at each other."

Gellie buttons the shirt and puts her hands together under the creases in her knees to warm them. "I'm really sorry that they aren't living together, your mom and dad. My parents are a pain in the neck, and they never even really talk to each other, but if they split . . . stopped living together, I'd be bummed, anyway. I really liked the way your parents were together. And if I'm sad, I'd think you'd be, too. So. Anyway."

"Thanks," I say. My heart feels really sore. I wonder if I'm going to have a heart attack or something. I want to keep talking about this, but I don't know what to say. I look at the Jintucket River and watch the big branches caught up in the runoff going south toward the sea. They are going fast. I imagine putting Mom and Dad carefully on branches and watching them float away.

We walk along the canal and cut up Prospect Street, then almost double back when we get to El Dorado. I climb up the maple tree and open the window, letting myself in slowly and quietly.

"Dad," I call. I don't hear anything. The apartment is dark and cold. I look into all four Zen-like empty rooms and go to the front door where Gellie is waiting to be let in. She drops her bag and her guitar and promptly lies down on Izzie's fake leopard-skin rug. It's more like a flat stuffed animal than a rug. I've loved it since I was a little kid. It has a big friendly head, and its mouth isn't open the way real animal-skin rugs always are. My dad said his parents had a bearskin in their living room until Aunt Izzie stepped into its open mouth and punctured her foot. My dad and his best friend took a hammer and knocked out all the teeth.

There are glass vases full of coral- and salmon-colored pebbles all over the living room. On the thick windowsill between the kitchen and living room, there is a statue of Buddha. I go into the kitchen and open a can of soup, dump it into a Pyrex measuring cup, and heat it up in the microwave. I pour the soup into two of Aunt Izzie's home-made clay bowls. We sit on the rug and sip. It warms me inside and I feel it seep through my whole body, heating me all the way to my cold damp toes. I look up at Aunt Izzie's big chrome clock, the size of the lid of a garbage can. It fills one whole wall. It has no numbers, but I think it's two-thirty.

"Sometimes I think it's because of me that Dad and Mom split up," I say, not taking my eyes off the big clock.

"Why?" she says.

"Because. All the stuff Mom said about how Dad needed to be home more to be there for me, to go to my school concerts, to help me with my homework, to give me guitar lessons. It's easier for two people to figure stuff out together than three. I get in the way."

"No, Randi," says Gellie. "Your mom wanted your dad home because she wanted him home. She just used you as an excuse. That's what we are. Big excuses for them to do whatever it is they want to do."

"Like being a model or a Hollywood star."

"Yup," says Gellie. "Let's make another deal. I won't be a Hollywood star to make my mother happy, and you won't be the reason your parents have problems. Deal?"

"Deal," I say.

We finish our soup and put the mugs in the sink. She follows me into the guest room. We climb into our beds without even taking off our clothes. I lie awake for a few minutes. My new song for Gellie is pounding away in my head. I squinch my eyes closed, but it is demanding to be sung.

"Are you awake?"

Gellie groans. "No!"

"I have to play you something." And I get my guitar from the other room and come back, sitting cross-legged on the bed.

You came by in the hat your mother knit you,
In clothes that do not fit you anymore.
You sat down in the corner of my bedroom,
I hung the Closed for Good sign on my door.

I have my eyes closed, partly because I'm tired, but partly because I'm scared to look Gellie in the eye. It's really weird to sing a song to the person you wrote it about.

I said, "Nothing works today. Everything is broken
Everything is choking on ambivalence."

You put a plastic angel on my desk and said, "I cannot
*   fix this*
But this may help to move you toward deliverance."

Glow-in-the-dark plastic angel, it's the first day of spring.
Nothing's making sense anymore,
Seventy-five miles an hour, let freedom ring,
I finally get what my wings are for,
I finally get what my wings are for.

I sing the verse about my parents. It hurts to sing it, but
I get through it.

All day long Mom and Dad were fighting,
Thunder and lightning through the walls.
Sticks and stones can break a heart to pieces
But it's nothing like the damage from no phone calls.
I wish that I could speak,
I'd tell her not to bother,
I'd tell her he's my father, not the king.
I wish that he would stay
But he won't be held by duty,
I wish he saw the beauty in the ring.

Then my new last verse:

You came by when everything was broken
Bringing me this token of your love.

You laughed and said, "It's only superstition
But I'm making it my mission to relieve you of
This tired broken world.
There's just no way to fight it,
Sit down, and be quiet, I won't go.
Here's an angel for your desk,
It's only a reminder;
I'm leaving her behind so you will always know I'm here."

I sing the chorus one last time. Gellie joins in on a harmony. I open my eyes and she is crying. When we finish the song, I just sit for a minute.

"Yeah," she says finally. "That was good."

CHAPTER NINETEEN

Pictures on Milk cartons

It's morning, and the sun is streaming through the sky-lights in the studio. We're sitting around Aunt Izzie's low coffee table, drinking tea and eating currant scones with bowls of lemon yogurt, which we picked up at the corner store. That cost us seven dollars. I still have money left from what John gave me. I keep expecting Dad to walk in any minute, and I've carefully rehearsed what I'll say when he does. It'll go like this:

Dad: Randi! What are you doing here?
Me: What does it look like I'm doing, man? I'm jamming.

Dad: Your mother and I have been worried sick about you! In fact, we've been crying so hard, we've been driven back into each other's arms, and that got us to talking, and now we're thinking about getting back together. All because of you. But that doesn't mean you're not in big fat trouble, young lady! We've decided to punish you by not letting you see Shawna again, ever! How does that sound?

Me (pretending to be horrified): Oh, no, Dad! Anything but that!

Dad: I'm sorry, Randi, but if we don't exact a really harsh punishment, you'll never learn.

Me: Oh, OK. I guess I really do have to learn my lesson.

Dad: Good. Now. Let me hear the songs you two have been working on.

And then Dad listens to us and tells us we're so good he's going to record a CD for us. And John's going to play backup guitar. Not a bad fantasy, huh?

But the morning passes and Dad doesn't show. We go out for lunch, taking our guitars with us to play on the corner of Main and Jeremy Newborn streets for passing change. When we get back to Aunt Izzie's, we see my mother's car pulling away. We duck quickly into the alley between Aunt Izzie's and the corner store where we'd gotten our scones. I watch my mother's taillights and get a flash of relief that I didn't see her face. If I had, I'd have to turn myself in, I think as we step inside.

"What are we going to do about the fact that my mother came here looking for us?" I say to Gellie. "We're not safe."

"Why not? If she came here once and didn't find us, that'll be it. She'll give up."

"Are you kidding? They're not going to give up! We're their daughters! They're going to think we're dead or something."

"Cool," says Gellie. "Maybe they'll have a funeral, and we can go eavesdrop like Jim and Huck Finn."

"Yeah." I chuckle, but I actually feel pretty bad about this. I suddenly picture Mom opening my bedroom door the morning after I left and, seeing I am missing, collapsing on the bed in tears. She would pick up each of my stuffed animals, one by one, and look into its glassy eyes and say, "Why? Why?" and then cling to it and sob. I close my eyes and shake this thought away. If I get soft, I won't be able to make it until Friday when we have our gig. I just have to make it till Friday.

"We'd better be careful about going out," says Gellie. "They probably have our pictures out on flyers and milk cartons and we'll get recognized and" — here she opens her eyes up really big — "*deported back to the Motherland.*"

"Hmm," I say. "Let's call Duge and get him to bring us some food. We're running out of money."

But Duge isn't home when we call and I don't want to leave a message because then his mother might hear it and call our moms.

"Maybe we'd better rethink this," I say, pacing around Aunt Izzie's apartment.

"Why?" says Gellie. "I've written three songs since I've been here."

Gellie's taking this we-make-the-rules thing a little too far if you ask me. I'm not used to her being braver than me. On the other hand, I'm not so eager to resurface. I'm beginning to think that if we do, we're going to be in really big trouble and that my punishment might be a tiny bit more severe than not getting to see Shawna.

I turn on the TV, expecting to see our faces on the local news. I listen to the radio, thinking I'll hear about two teenage girls with guitars who are missing. Nothing. Maybe they're glad we're gone. It's like our fear fantasy from fifth grade come true, the one where the reason our mothers are late picking us up is because they never wanted us and always planned to abandon us someday.

☆ ☆ ☆

I am lying in bed with my eyes closed, kind of dozing but not really. I've been thinking about bad guys coming into the apartment or Dad coming in and finding us and sending us back to Mrs. Riddle, who in my four A.M. mind is about three times her normal size and has gigantic long teeth and snakes for hair.

"Nothing personal," I murmur out loud to Dad, who has come to sit on the end of my bed and mope. "I love your songs. But you can't compare playing someone else's songs to playing your own."

He looks at me and then, to my surprise, nods in agreement. "That is the secret I've been afraid to admit to anyone, most of all myself. Don't you ever stop performing your own songs. I wish I hadn't."

Before I can remind my dad that he still does perform his own songs, at least sometimes, I hear a noise in the hallway outside the apartment door. I sit bolt upright and listen. Dad is no longer at the foot of my bed. Streetlamp light shines in and I am 100 percent awake. I hear, "Lordy Mother of Heaven! What in Hades is going on here?" I bound out of bed and into the living room where I see Aunt Izzie standing in the half-open door to the apartment, several shopping bags in her hand along with her suitcase and her big bloodhound, Kramer, on a leash.

"What are you doing back so soon?" I say, looking around quickly to assess the damage she'll catch right off the bat.

"Oh, Randi! Girls! Thank God you are OK." And she drops everything and races over to hug me. I melt in her arms and feel totally relaxed, until I register the blow to my head with her soft felt hat.

"What in tarnation did you think you were doing? Do you have any idea how crazed with worry we all were about you? What am I doing? I need to call your parents right away."

"No!" Gellie and I holler in unison.

"Please, Aunt Izzie, please don't! They'll kill us," I say.

"As well they should," says Aunt Izzie, picking up the phone.

"Wait!" says Gellie. "It's four in the morning. They're all asleep! Can't you just let us say one thing before you wake them? What difference can a couple of hours make?"

And Aunt Izzie, bless her old radical sixties heart, pauses and, with a sigh, hangs up the phone.

"OK, I'll wait," she says. "But you have to tell me the whole story."

The sun is coming up, and we are eating the pancakes and fresh eggs Aunt Izzie made us. We've told her everything, and she's listened and nodded and even asked to hear us sing.

"What I don't get is why you can't just tell your mother you don't want to be a model anymore," says Aunt Izzie, drinking tea.

"Because," says Gellie.

"She did!" I interrupt. "I told you! She *said* she didn't want to be in the dinosaur movie and that she wanted to sing with me and stay in school and be normal!"

Aunt Izzie looks completely unimpressed. "Well, Gellie?"

Gellie puts her chin on her palm and leans her elbow on the table, covering her mouth with her hand.

She's thinking this over?

"They kidnapped her!" I shout. "I saw it! It was like a gangster movie!"

Aunt Izzie is quiet. "This is really about Gellie and *her*

choices," she says. "Gellie is a free person. What did you say when they put you in the car like that?"

Gellie continues to sit with her hand covering her mouth, but I see what might be tears forming in her eyes. Fascinated, I watch as they get bigger and bigger and more undeniably tearlike and eventually spill onto and over her arm like a waterfall.

"I caved," she finally says. "I said I'd do what they wanted. And the truth is . . . Randi, don't be mad, but sometimes I do want it."

Aunt Izzie gets up and goes over to where Gellie is sitting and puts her arms around Gellie's head, holding it to her belly. Gellie sobs.

"What did they say to you in the car, honey?"

"They said . . . ," Gellie is crying so hard, it's not easy to understand. "Mom said, 'You won't always be this young, this small. You're going to grow up, and when that happens, there's no turning back. When you have a child of your own, you won't get to have the luxury of saying no to opportunities like this. Because no one will ever offer you any. Your whole life will be one big NO.'"

Aunt Izzie keeps holding Gellie. Gellie cries some more, and I think about leaving the room, but part of me wants to join in the hug fest. Instead I just sit on the couch feeling big and clumsy.

"You can be a model, too," I mutter. "I'm not mad."

Gellie blows her nose. "I really don't want to do this movie. I'm not saying I don't ever want to do anything

Boo and Steve set up ever again, but I want to be the one to decide. I want to sing with you. I want to go to school. And that's pretty much enough."

And she looks over at me, and her face, all red and tearstained, breaks into a big wet smile.

Aunt Izzie nods. "Let's tell them, then." And she looks for the phone, which I'd hidden under a couch cushion. I pull it out and hand it to her.

"Here," I say. "Call my parents first."

"Well, actually," says Aunt Izzie, her mouth curling into a smile, "they already know you're here."

"What?" we say together.

"Your mom thought you'd come here first thing when she woke up and found you gone. She was so sure that when Mrs. Riddle called her, hysterical, she said she knew you were safe and would get right back to her. Then she came over here, saw your Snoopy bag, and knew for sure."

"Why did she leave, then?" I ask, so amazed and angry and relieved that I'm almost sputtering. "Why didn't she stay and bust us?"

"Sweetheart," says Aunt Izzie gently, looking me in the eye. "She ran away, too. Remember?"

"Yeah, but —" I was about to say, "She ran away for real." How did she know *I* hadn't?

"She's been thinking about this ever since you were born. Kids often do the same thing their parents do. Call it cosmic karma. And she'd been thinking about how she wished her parents had reacted to her. Remember, they *disowned* her. That's not the kind of mother she wanted to be to you, Randi.

"Anyway, she came right over to your parents' house, Gellie, and she told your mother that you were fine, that you needed some time to think and straighten out your choices, that she was going to call me, and that I was going to fly home to be with you."

"And my mom bought that?" says Gellie doubtfully.

"Madeleine told your mother about how she had run away. She argued that if they came and dragged you home, you might run away again. That they needed to let you make up your own minds about some things and also to trust that home could be a safe place to be."

"And my mom said she'd let me make up my own mind?"

"Well," says Aunt Izzie. "She didn't quite have a choice. Apparently, when your father heard about the dinosaur movie, he put his foot down and said he wouldn't let you do that."

"My *father* said that?" Gellie is incredulous. So am I. I had no idea her father had any opinions about any of his daughters at all.

"Yes, he did. He said he wasn't about to let you sacrifice even one day of school to participate in such an idiotic enterprise. Your mother was apparently surprised into silence — at first, anyway. I think one of your sisters, or maybe both of them, ran some interference with your mom. At any rate, your parents agreed to let you stay here for a few days, though they've all come by to check up on you every few hours, just to make sure you're OK."

"They did?" I can't believe it. It's like that old song Dad used to sing to me, "Someone to Watch over Me." I realize I'm smiling. This is why there were no pictures on milk cartons.

CHAPTER TWENTY

Big Show at the
May Day café

The May Day Café is a hole-in-the-wall in the oldest, hippest, poorest part of town, an area called West Jintucket. It's a small performance space that serves really terrible health food and really good coffee. It is decorated with used books, which serve as a kind of library for the customers. In short, it could not be more un-Clairman.

It's a miracle that Mrs. Riddle agreed to let us play here tonight. I do know both of us are in hideous trouble and will probably be grounded for the rest of our teenage years.

☆ ☆ ☆

My parents had come to Aunt Izzie's in the same car; Barbara came with Mrs. Riddle. When Mom and Dad came into the apartment, I sensed something had changed between them. Call it wishful thinking, but it really felt as if they were a united front.

"Oh, sweetheart." Mom buried her face in my hair. "I love you so much. Don't ever do that again!" She pulled her head out of my neck and looked me in the eye. "You really need to talk to me when you're angry."

"I wasn't exactly angry," I said, feeling kind of angry. "I was helping Gellie."

Dad seemed more shaken up. "You really frightened us, Randi. Almost anything you do is OK, but this was not OK. This is NOT OK."

I know he still loves me and all, but this reaction scared me, and I imagine it'll be enough to keep me on good behavior for the next few years.

Mrs. Riddle was practically hysterical. "What did you think you were doing?" she yelled at me. "I forbid you ever to fraternize with my daughter again!"

"Mom, chill," said Barbara. "It's not Randi's fault. Gellie is her own person."

"Mom!" said Gellie. "I can't take this anymore! I need to live my own life. Sometimes I feel like you want me to do this because you never had your chance to shine again after I was born. I don't always want to do what you want me to do. I need to have a life outside of your ideas for me. Margie and Barbara got to have friends and do things just for fun. I want that, too. I want to have hobbies. I don't care if that means I never get famous."

"Yeah, Mom, what's so wrong with that?" said Barbara, hands on her hips like a good defense-lawyer-to-be. "She's finally getting off the Geek of the Week list after ten years of complete nerd-dom. You should be celebrating."

"But Gellie's going to be famous!" Mrs. Riddle wailed. "We've worked and worked our whole lives for this, honey. How can you throw it all out the window? How can you throw all my work for you back in my face? All I've ever wanted for you is the very best! I want you to be a star! *We are so close to it!*"

Then Gellie said, very softly and gently, "Mom, maybe *you* should be the actress."

Mrs. Riddle's face turned purple and I thought she was going to spontaneously combust. But instead she sank into Aunt Izzie's couch. "It's too late," she said quietly and in a voice that sounded much younger than she is.

We all looked at her. Barbara mouthed, "Oh, God" and rolled her eyes and walked into Aunt Izzie's kitchen. Mom opened her mouth and then closed it. She went over and sat down next to Mrs. Riddle and put an arm tentatively around her shoulder.

"No, it's not, June. I thought the same thing about myself a couple of years ago. I thought it was too late for me to do anything other than be a mom to Randi and a wife to a traveling musician. And now I have this whole new life. It's not perfect, and I'm not leaping tall buildings in a single bound, but I am doing something that I like and that I believe makes a difference. And I have my own room with a door that I can close behind me. I can put food on the table for my family."

It's not like after that Mrs. Riddle jumped up and said, "Eureka! That's just what I'm going to do! I'll go be the new Palmolive lady and be in my own commercials!" But something in what Mom said seemed to quiet her. Either that or she was just very, very tired. But she said Gellie could do the show tonight, and the next day they'd talk about consequences.

The Riddles returned to Clairman to have lunch. I knew Gellie would be in Jintucket for the gig; Barbara swore she'd be responsible for getting her there.

Aunt Izzie and Mom went to the deli around the corner to get us sandwiches for lunch. While they were gone, Dad cleared his throat and said, "I have a new song. I'd like to play it for you."

I couldn't believe it. Dad is always pestering Mom to listen to his songs, but this was the first time he'd ever asked me to hear a song.

"You know how you're always on my case to write from my own point of view?" he said.

"Yeah." My heart was racing. I don't know why.

"Well. You gave me a reason to do that."

And he took the Gibson I got for Gellie and played me a song about a father and a daughter who used to share music with each other, but now the girl is growing up, changing, not interested in her dad anymore. I was amazed and flattered and sorry for Dad and embarrassed, all at the same time. Dad was singing, "la la la" in the middle of the song. He had his eyes closed. I was glad. This was excruciating. I always thought I'd love it if Dad wrote a song for me. Now I wasn't so convinced. I felt like a butterfly under a microscope. I didn't know how to react.

He continued. In the song, the girl asks her dad to take her to a show by a musician she likes. He does, and he suddenly understands that she really hasn't left him at all. The girl in the song says, "I always knew there would be a road back to here."

Dad sang:

Beautiful, my little Glory
You'll always be my baby girl
I am following your story
I am leaving you the world.

He finished and I didn't look up. "Thanks," I muttered. "That's a good song." But I felt almost as great as I feel when I am the one performing. I felt seen.

Dad cleared his throat again, laying the guitar sideways on his lap.

"Randi," he said. "Your mom's right about one thing. I'm not around enough for you."

"Yes, you are!" I said hotly. "You're around plenty!"

"No. I mean. Well. Put it this way: I'm not around *you* as much as *I'd* like to be. And that's my job. But your job is to grow up and get away from me, not the other way around. OK? Does that make sense?"

Before I could answer, Mom and Izzie came back in.

"Who wants sandwiches?" Mom called. "I got sun-dried tomato and Brie. Or else tuna wasabi. Any takers?"

Dad leaned in and said in a low voice. "From now on, I want *you* to fit *me* into your schedule. Not the other way around."

And I didn't say anything, but I put my arms around him and let him hug me for a long, long time.

"Where was Dad for the last few days, anyway?" I asked Mom when Dad went out to get the car after lunch. "I kept expecting him to come here."

"He came home," Mom said, not looking at me. "I needed him."

☆ ☆ ☆

It's Dad's birthday. After the show, we're going to have a party back home. Just Mom, Dad, and me. I'll give Dad the stash of CDs I've been collecting all summer. I didn't ask if he's going to spend the night tonight. I don't need to know everything right away.

He sent Gellie and me a dozen white roses. When we arrived at the club, they were in the dressing room on the table in front of the mirror with this card:

Girls—
Congratulations on your very first gig. You will always remember this night. Other things to

remember: tell it like it is, be true to yourself, and if you get stage fright, picture the audience in their underwear. Break a leg.

Love,

Dad

P.S. Don't *ever* eat the food the club serves you.

I'm wearing a green button-down shirt, black pants, and platform shoes. I think I look like Rhodie Becket. Gellie is wearing yellow suede bell-bottoms, her velvet shirt, and underneath that, an orange T-shirt Margie gave her that says BITE ME. Mrs. Riddle is going to have a cow when she sees it. Gellie and I peek behind the dressing room door, which is really just a curtain, to see where our families are. I see Dr. Riddle, who brought his copy of the Clairman *Observer* and is currently poring over it, sitting at a table with Margie and Jeremy and Barbara. All my friends are at the show. That means Shawna is *not* at the show, thank God, though I have to admit, I am a little disappointed. It would have been fun to sing "Clairman Town" right at Shawna. Attack her where she lives! Combat songwriting! That's what Gellie and I call it. "The guitar is mightier than the Uzi," Gellie intones.

My real friends are here. Duge has set up a tripod and is going to make a video of us. John's here, and he even checked out the dressing room to make sure everything was all set. And Essie is coming in with Martin and Derek. I feel nervous just seeing them, but this is what I always wanted: for the cool kids at school to see me doing what only I can do.

Mrs. Riddle is coming from the back of the room with Boo and Steve. She looks a little more like her old self, her head high, tossing her thick hair around.

"Oh, no," I shudder, imagining another kidnapping.

Gellie shrugs. "Don't worry. I think she's just switched from being my modeling–TV star cheerleader to being my singer–songwriter cheerleader. She just wants to show me off. I think she's decided that she's not that particular what the arena is."

That doesn't exactly reassure me. I have visions of Mrs. Riddle trying to get us gigs, telling us what to wear, how to do our hair. But, then, that will be tomorrow's problem. And I have choices. We have choices. We can say no.

Of course, Aunt Izzie is here, in the front row. I think she persuaded possibly every student she's ever taught to come tonight. "You have to see my girls," she says when we come out to greet everyone a half hour before we go on. She puts her hands on each of our heads, and Gellie puts her arms around Aunt Izzie's waist.

Izzie and Gellie are going to have lunch together once a month. I thought it would bother me, and maybe it did a little this morning when I first heard of the plan, but tonight I'm thinking that nothing could be better than having all these cool people that I like so much get to know each other better. And that's what they're doing. John is talking to my mom. Barbara is over at Aunt Izzie's table now, leaning over the back of a chair. Duge is asking Dad about his recording setup. And tonight everyone's going to hear us sing. Everyone's going to hear us sing songs we wrote.

Lydia, the owner, the ex-girlfriend of John, comes into the dressing room. "This is a great crowd, girls," she says. "I don't usually see this with first-timers. If you're halfway decent, I'll book you back once a month."

"Really?" I say. Gellie and I look at each other as if we've just won an Oscar.

"*If* you're decent," she repeats with a smile. "And from the sound of your tape, you should be." She turns to go, and Gellie and I make the silent-scream face. Gellie gets up and peeks through the curtain to spy on the audience again. She turns around, white-faced, wide-eyed.

"I think Rhodie Becket's here," she whispers. "Oh, my God! I'm going to die! She's going to see me play her guitar! What if she wants it back!"

"Then she'll have to fight you for it," I say, though the idea of Rhodie seeing us play makes me want to stand up about six inches taller. "We're going to blow her away!"

Gellie pulls the wooden box out of her bag and sets the glow-in-the-dark plastic angel on the coffee table. I wind it up. She shines the flashlight on it.

"May we kick ass," we intone in unison. We say the words slowly and in a deep voice.

Lydia comes back in with a bouquet of daisies.

"This is from a gentleman fan," she says. The card says,

Remember us little guys who believed in you from the beginning. You two are my Big Idea.

Your devoted fan and friend,

Duge

"I told him I'd meet him tomorrow in the lighting booth at school," says Gellie, examining the card a little too carefully. "He's going to give me lessons on how to get along with The Tribe without being a total sellout. It can't hurt. I need all the help I can get."

Lydia pokes her head back in. "Five minutes," she says and leaves us alone. We rush to the mirror to put the finishing touches on our makeup.

Gellie and I stand looking at each other's face in the mirror. Today we each make the other one look beautiful. My face is long and angular, and I'm having a good-eye day, meaning they aren't all puffy like they can get sometimes. My skin looks all glowy and shiny and tight across my nose. Gellie's face looks golden and heart-shaped as usual, but she's got a spark in her eye and looks commanding. I open my mouth to say something — I don't even know what — and Gellie shakes her head and smiles. She takes my hand. We stand there for a minute, maybe two. Maybe five.

Finally, she turns to face me, and I see my face reflected in her watermelon-seed eyes. I look like a person you could trust. She grins.

"Let's go," she says.